NOAH AND NAAMAH

GREAT ROMANCES OF THE BIBLE SERIES

RENA JONES

LOPER PUBLISHING

CONTENTS

PROLOGUE – WHEN THE WORLD TURNED AWAY

In the beginning, the earth was new and unspoiled. The rivers sang with life, the trees lifted their arms in praise, and men walked with the memory of Eden still burning in their hearts. The stories of Adam and the garden were not yet legend but history — told at firesides by men whose fathers had known him face to face.

For a time, the sons of men remembered their Maker. They built altars of stone and called on His name. The world prospered under the blessing spoken in Eden: *Be fruitful and fill the earth.* And fill it they did.

But as the generations passed, the sound of prayer grew faint beneath the noise of pride. Men learned to build cities, to forge metal from the earth, to make instruments of both music and war. The earth grew crowded with their works — and empty of their reverence.

Then came the Watchers, the heavenly ones who forsook their place. They descended under starlight, beautiful and terrible, teaching men arts never meant for mortal hands. From them came the mighty ones — the Nephilim — giants in stature, fierce in appetite, worshiped as gods by those who had forgotten the true One.

The hearts of men turned fully to corruption. Blood filled the soil. Women were taken by force. Children were raised to serve violence. The very air trembled with defiance against Heaven.

Yet in the midst of that ruin, there remained a few who still walked in the old ways — who remembered the words of Adam and the promise of the Creator. Among them were the descendants of Seth, keepers of the sacred history, whose tents lay far from the cities of the fallen ones.

And in one of those tents, a man named **Noah**, son of **Lamech**, was being prepared for a purpose the world could not yet imagine.

The season was turning. The age of innocence was ending. And the first rumblings of judgment could already be felt upon the wind.

CHAPTER ONE

NIGHT OF ASHES

S moke moved like a living thing through the palms, tasting the air and finding every throat. Naamah pressed her face to the earth and breathed through the veil clutched in her fist. The veil smelled of cedar and the oil her mother used to smooth her hair; now it smelled of cinders.

The giants had come at dusk, when shadows made all men smaller. Their laughter had rolled over the village like thunder, followed by the crack of beams and the startled cries of goats. Women were dragged to the square and bound to the half-fallen sycamore. Men who rushed forward were flung aside as if they were reeds. The Nephilim moved without hurry, their wrists encircled with bands of hammered iron that caught and threw the firelight. One of them—broad-shouldered, ash-faced—tied Naamah's mother near the roots and marked her with a smear of pitch as though she were spoil.

"Do not speak," Naamah had mouthed, head barely lifted from the dust. Her mother's eyes—brave, wet—found her under the broken loom and held her there with a silent command: **Live.**

Naamah had not moved since. Not when a child wailed for its father. Not when the giants kicked apart the bread-oven for sport. Not when a torch licked up the side of her own tent and the wool coverlet caught and curled like leaves in a kiln. She had only stayed and breathed and prayed into the dirt: *God of my mother and of Adam before her, see us. Remember us.*

A hiss broke the din, soft as a cricket. Another answered from the darkness beyond the goat-pen.

Naamah flattened her hand and felt it: the thud of many feet, not heavy as the giants', but quick, careful, measured. A shadow slid across what was left of her threshold, then stilled. Another followed, pausing where the light was deepest, then melting into the gap between the dye-pots. They were men—five, perhaps six—moving without torches, eyes down, breath short.

The first of them passed so near Naamah could have touched his heel. He was tall, not like the Nephilim—no man was—but taller than her father had been, broad through the shoulders. He wore no iron, only leather, and his hair was bound away from his face with a strip of twisted flax. In his hand a knife gleamed dull, its edge darkened with soot. He knelt to the split beam, slid the blade under a binding, and eased it through without a sound. When he lifted his head, for an instant the fire found his eyes.

They were clear. Not hard, not reckless. Clear, as if a river ran behind them.

He saw her.

Not the whole of her—only the shape of a girl lying flat in the dust with a strip of veil crushed to her lips. His gaze did not startle or wander. It held. It asked nothing, and promised nothing, and yet Naamah felt a steadiness move through her like cool water. He touched two fingers to the ground—*stay*—and was gone.

They moved like that: shadows sewn to the torn edges of her life. One cut the tethering line to the animal pen so the goats would drift to the far side and bleat there, drawing a guard away. Another tipped a basket with a nudge of his knee so its spill of shells rolled into the dark under the collapsed awning, where curious hands would think to follow. A third raised a palm toward the open square and waited, counting the pace of the giant who circled, head bent, idly humming the false song the Watchers taught.

When the steps passed, he slipped to the sycamore and crouched at the first woman's wrists.

Naamah risked a look toward her mother. Pitch glistened on the older woman's cheek like a black tear. The giant's mark.

A sudden roar from the far edge of the village—goats panicked, clattering into the pottery racks. Shouts. The guard nearest the tree broke from his post and ran toward the noise, dragging his spear. The others laughed and turned to watch as jars burst like fruit on stone.

The tall man was up and moving. He crossed open ground in three long strides, dropped to a knee, and sliced through two bindings before the second woman even realized the cord had snapped. He pressed a finger to her lips and tipped his head toward the shadowed alley. She went, stumbling. Another binding. Another woman gone, legs weak but willing. He worked left to right, efficient, never looking at the fire, not once glancing at the giants whose heads turned toward the commotion he and his men had planned.

Then he reached Naamah's mother.

The pitch-mark shone. The rope at her wrists had been pulled cruelly tight. She lifted her chin as the stranger came, as if to make his work easier, as if she had decided already to belong to freedom and would not let fear shame her. The knife bit; the rope loosened.

Naamah's mother did not flee. She shook her head toward the burned tent, toward the loom's black ribs, toward the patch of earth where a daughter lay hidden.

He looked that way, just once.

Naamah's heart beat a warning against the earth. *No—no—go. Take her. Leave me. Go.*

He made a sign with his hand that she did not know but somehow understood: *I see.*

A shout cracked the air—one of the giants had found the bedded goats and flung a kid into the night. The little body struck a clay wall and slid. Laughter followed, hot and mean. The running guard turned back, impatient, sweeping the square with his spear. He saw the movement at the sycamore and bellowed.

"Now," hissed a voice from the dark.

Everything quickened. The stranger's men appeared where a heartbeat earlier there had been only shadow. Two flanked the returning guard and let him pass between them, then tripped and bound his ankles with the same cord they had cut from the women. A third tossed a sling—there was a soft thump, and the giant's torch spun into the dust. Dimness swallowed the sycamore.

Naamah was already moving.

Her legs were stiff as kilnwood, but fear made them nimble. She slid from the broken tent and kept to the line of fallen beams. In the half-light the stranger was a smudge of motion and breath, a murmur of quiet orders. He placed Naamah's mother's hand against the back of a fleeing woman and gave it a push. Then he turned to the burnt edge of the camp—exactly where Naamah had to cross open ground if she wanted to reach him.

They saw each other fully then, not as a hidden girl and a passing shadow, but as two souls thrown into the same narrow moment. He had ash across one cheek. He wore no ornaments, nothing to catch flame. A line—perhaps a scar—ran along his forearm like a deliberate mark. He looked at Naamah as he had before: steady, clear.

She rose. He lifted a hand—*wait*—then set his eyes on the nearest giant. The ash-faced one had returned and was squinting into the square, puzzled by the sudden thinning of captives. His lips peeled back from his teeth. His hand closed on the shaft of his spear.

"Left," the stranger breathed, though there was no one at his side. From the left, a stone sang. It struck the iron band on the giant's wrist with a sound like a chime, and in his surprise his grip faltered. The spear's point dipped. The stranger made a sign, swift as a bird's wing.

Now.

Naamah ran.

The world narrowed to the rhythm of her feet and the white of his eyes. She felt the heat of the dying oven on one side, the scrape of a broken axle on her calf, the way the ground rose slightly where the running water always cut a channel in spring. The giant's attention went with the stone's echo; he turned his head like an ox hearing its name. Naamah passed the open place and fell into the shadow at the stranger's feet.

He caught her by the shoulders—not roughly, but firmly, as though anchoring a tent-rope in a sudden wind. For a heartbeat they were very close, the smoke between them, her breath loud in her own ears. He smelled of cedar and leather and something clean she could not name in a night like this.

"Your mother?" he whispered.

"Free," Naamah managed. "She went with the others."

"Good." He released her, and in the release there was no panic, only a sense—strange in a night of terror—of order. "Can you run?"

"Yes."

"Then take this way," he said, angling her toward a path that felt invisible until he pointed. "Keep the burnt wall to your right hand. When you reach water, follow it upstream. Our men wait where the tamarisks bend. If anyone touches you, cry like a nightbird."

"What sound is that?" Her voice surprised her—calm, almost curious. Fear could not imagine nightbirds.

He made it then, soft in his throat, a rising whistle followed by a click of tongue. It was not beautiful, but the shape of it settled in her. She nodded.

A shout rose—"Here! Here!"—and the ash-faced giant lumbered toward them, finally seeing what he had not wished to see: women vanishing like dew, a man he did not know standing where no man should stand.

The stranger pushed Naamah gently and stepped out of shadow.

"Go," he said, and there was iron in that single word, more than the giants wore.

Naamah went. The world opened into a lane torn by cart wheels. Firelight flapped at her back; ahead, darkness accepted her. The sounds of the square dimmed, then flared, then dimmed again as if the village itself breathed.

Behind her, the clash of action: a grunt, a dull thud, the wet rip of a rope, men's feet moving exactly where they had meant to be all along. Once—only once—she looked back. The stranger had no spear; the one he had pulled from the dust had snapped against the giant's wrist-band, and he did not waste a heartbeat cursing it. He moved instead, drawing the giant past the fallen axle where two of his men lay flat as stones. They rose and caught the giant by the knees like a pair of hunters felling a bull. The ash-faced one crashed to the earth and bellowed, sending crows from the date palms.

Naamah turned again and ran.

The burnt wall rasped her palm as she slid along it. The pool at the end of the lane flashed like a fallen star—she found the trickle that fed it and plunged into reeds taller than herself. Frogs scattered. Mud took her feet and released them. She followed the stream until the palms thinned and the tamarisks gathered, whispering.

A hand lifted in the gloom. "Here," a voice murmured, low and warm. Two women reached out, pulled Naamah into a knot of breath and shoulders and hot, grateful hands. Her mother was there—*blessed God, she was there*—and they clung for an instant that belonged to no Watcher, no giant, no man. It belonged to the One who made breath.

"We will count," said the warm voice, "and when we are full, we will go."

Naamah tried to count but numbers fell apart in her head. She only listened—to the cries in the far square, to the nightbird calling and being answered from the broken places, to her mother's heart under her cheek. She listened, too, for the new sound she did not yet know she knew: the cadence of the stranger's words as he ordered his men and the shape of his breathing when he ran.

They came in pairs and threes from every slashed alley: soot-faced, weeping, silent, clutching children, clutching nothing. A girl younger than Naamah had blood on her foot and did not seem to notice. An elder with hair like cloud had two black crescents burned into her palms where rope had bitten. They settled in the reeds, the murmur of their relief sharper than their fear had been.

Then the nightbird called twice and fell still.

The warm-voiced man—one of the rescuers—lifted his head. "We move," he said, and touched the nearest shoulder, then the next.

They rose, a chain of shadows. Naamah took her mother's hand and followed. The stream turned to a shallow run where the earth dipped; they waded, water closing around their ankles, the mud mercifully quiet under their feet. Tamarisk branches brushed their hair, laid cool fronds on hot cheeks, then opened to a strip of lowland where the land lifted gently away from the blaze behind.

They had almost reached the first fold of safety when Naamah heard it: feet that did not belong to their line. Heavy. Eager. Fast.

"Down," the warm voice hissed.

They melted to the earth, faces in the wild thyme. The heavy steps drew near, then slowed, then stopped. Naamah tasted the metal at the back of her tongue that comes blood from biting her tongue.

"Rise," said another voice, clear and close, and Naamah knew it before she knew she knew it. "Rise and keep moving."

The stranger stepped into the strip of stars.

He had a woman on his back—small, unconscious, arms dangling—and another man at his side whose breath came ragged and wet. Two of his company flanked them, scanning the dark. The heaviness Naamah had heard was not pursuit. It was the weight of those they would not leave.

He lowered the woman to the arms that reached for her, nodded once, and turned his face toward the direction of the village. Firelight tinted his jaw. For the first time she saw the whole of him: not the steadiness only, but the cost of it—sweat streaked with ash, a bruise coming up under one eye, hands nicked where rope and stone had taken their tithe. He looked at the line of women, at Naamah, at the old and the little ones, and a looseness came into his shoulders—not weariness, exactly, but the easing a man allows himself when something he dared has not failed.

"Our path bends west to the ridge," he said quietly. "We go by the sheep-steps. There is water there, and men who will guard you through the night."

The warm-voiced rescuer touched his forearm. "Noah," he said, "we counted thirty. We thought we would bring twenty."

"God gave thirty," the stranger answered. "We take thirty."

Naamah did not mean to speak, but the name shaped itself before she could stop it. "Noah."

His eyes found her in the low light. Surprise passed over his face—not at being known, but at being called by a girl he had not met. He inclined his head once, not proud, not shy. "Come," he said, and turned to lead them.

They went as he said, by the sheep-steps that a shepherd knows even in the dark. The ridge lifted them into a wind that brought the smell of clean rock and distance. Behind, the village's glow throbbed and faded with the turns of the land until it was only a smear on the horizon, and then not even that.

At the crest, where the path split and the tamarisks gave way to scrub, a ring of men waited. They were not many, but they stood like a wall. They had water-skins and cloaks and quiet voices. One of them—older, his beard shot with grey—took Noah's face gently in his hands and looked at him as a father looks when the son he sent returns with more than he dared hope.

"You were not seen?" the elder asked.

"We were seen," Noah said. His mouth twitched as if with a private thought. "But not understood."

The elder's eyes lifted to the line of women, to the children pressed to skirts, to Naamah's mother's marked cheek. His jaw set. Then, softening, he opened his hands to the night and said, "Blessed be the Name who sees."

Naamah and her mother sank onto a folded cloak. Water went into their hands; bread followed, coarse and honest. Naamah ate because her body asked for it, not because she understood she was safe. Her eyes found Noah even when she told them not to. He moved among the rescued without ceremony, taking count again, tying a strip of linen around a barefoot child's cut, lifting a jar for an old woman whose arms shook. When he came to Naamah and her mother, he paused.

"You kept the path," he said to Naamah in that steady way of his, as though stating a small fact was the same as offering thanks.

"You made it plain," she answered, and then wondered at herself for saying it.

His gaze warmed, just a shade. He looked to her mother. "Lady, the mark upon you—does it burn?"

"It is only pitch," her mother said, wiping at it with the side of her hand. "It stings less than the thought of those who did it."

"We will wash it away before dawn," Noah said. "Some stains do not belong to those who wear them."

He rose to go and then, as though remembering something that had waited in him all along, added, "At first light we will take you farther—beyond the reach of tonight's anger. There is a tented place where men still call on the Creator. You may rest there as long as you wish."

Naamah's mother bowed her head in thanks. Naamah found she could not; the motion felt too great for her neck. She only looked at him, and the words came without design: "You were not afraid."

"I was afraid," he said simply. "But I feared the wrong thing more."

"What wrong thing?"

"That I would leave you to your enemies," he answered, and with that he moved on.

The night thinned. Somewhere below, jackals argued over what the giants left behind. A breeze threaded the ridge and combed Naamah's hair, lifting the singed ends. She lay back on the cloak and watched the sky's black loosen to blue. The world the elders spoke of in the old stories—the clean world, the praising world—felt far. And yet a new thing lay near: a name, a certainty, a voice that had stood between her and ruin and said *Go*, and the way her heart had obeyed without question.

In that first pale of morning, when birds tried their notes and failed and tried again, Naamah turned her face toward the man who had led them by the sheep-steps and whispered to herself, as if naming a seed you mean to keep watered:

"Noah."

CHAPTER TWO

THE MORNING AFTER

The night had been long, but morning came as it always had since the beginning, for the world was still veiled in its first mist. Dew clung to every blade of grass like scattered pearls, and a veil of vapor rose from the ground to soften the edges of the hills. Light seeped through the haze, gentle as breath, touching what ruin had not reached.

Naamah awoke to the sound of quiet voices and the crackle of a small fire. Her mother lay beside her, breathing evenly, her hand still clasped around Naamah's wrist as though she feared to let go even in sleep. Around them, women stirred on woven mats, the rescued of the night before, their faces streaked with soot and fatigue but alive.

The air smelled of herbs steeping in clay pots, and of bread being warmed on stones.

She pushed herself upright, wincing at the stiffness in her legs. The sight that met her eyes was unlike any she had known.

Men moved among the camp with measured calm. None shouted. None struck beasts to make them hurry. The younger ones worked in silence, tending the fires or bringing water from the low stream that wound through the meadow. When they passed one another, they nodded or spoke a blessing. The camp itself seemed alive with order—the kind that comes when peace is not weakness but strength.

Noah stood apart, near the edge of the stream, speaking with an older man whose hair was white as goat's milk and whose eyes held a depth that made her think of deep wells. He must be his father, she thought. The two stood like twin trees, one in full height, one in age-hollowed dignity. Between them passed words she could not hear, but she saw the concern in their faces. From time to time, Noah turned toward the ridge as though searching for a sign that danger might yet follow them.

When he saw her stir, his gaze lingered only a moment—steady, acknowledging, nothing more. Then he returned to his talk.

Naamah's mother rose, smoothing her singed dress. "They have given us water and food," she said softly. "And a place among their women until we are strong enough to travel. These are good people, Naamah. I did not think such men still lived upon the earth."

Naamah looked toward Noah again. "Who are they?"

"The line of Seth, so I am told," her mother answered. "They dwell apart from the sons of Cain, far from the cities. They keep the old ways, and the name of the Creator is still spoken in their tents."

Naamah lowered her eyes. "And the man who led us?"

Her mother hesitated, as if tasting the name. "Noah, son of Lamech. They say his forefathers walked with God, and that righteousness follows him as a shadow follows the sun."

Naamah touched the edge of her veil. "He risked his life for strangers."

"He risked it for what is right," her mother said, pouring warm water over her hands. "That is rarer than courage."

A woman approached carrying a bowl of crushed herbs and a strip of linen. She knelt before Naamah's mother and spoke gently. "For your burns. My name is Tiria." Her hair was plaited simply, her eyes kind. "You will stay here until your strength returns. Noah has said it."

"He commands much?" Naamah asked before she could stop herself.

Tiria smiled faintly. "He commands little. He asks, and men obey because they see God's favor in him. That is a different thing."

When she had gone, Naamah helped bind her mother's wrists and then wandered toward the stream, drawn by the low hum of men's voices. The mist drifted off the water in slow ribbons, and she saw the reflection of trees bend and sway as though they were listening.

Noah was there still, speaking with the white-haired man. His tunic was clean but frayed at the hem, his hands reddened from washing blood and ash from them. He looked older by years than he had the night before, though the morning light softened him. When he noticed her standing by the water, he inclined his head.

"You rested?"

"I did." Her voice faltered. "Because of you."

His expression did not change, yet something in his eyes eased. "It was not because of me. The Almighty gave us favor to do what was just."

Naamah hesitated, then said quietly, "You came when no one else would have dared."

He studied her for a heartbeat, then looked out over the meadow. "When men fear the wrong things, they grow smaller each day. Better to fear God and grow larger within."

She did not fully understand, but the calm in his tone steadied her. "Will you stay here long?" she asked.

"For a time," he said. "But the Nephilim will not forget what we took from them. We must move our tents before their wrath follows."

"Then my mother and I should go," she said quickly. "We will not bring danger upon your people."

Noah turned to her. "Danger is already upon the earth, Naamah. It walks in daylight now, not only in shadows. You and your mother are safer here than alone."

He bent to lift a jar from the stream. "Take this water back to the women. It will ease the smoke in their throats."

She took it, careful not to touch his hand, though her pulse quickened at the nearness. His calm was like the hush before dawn—neither cold nor distant, simply sure.

When she returned to her mother, the older woman was sitting beside Tiria, watching the men begin to take down a line of smaller tents. "They are preparing to move," Tiria explained. "Before midday we'll go toward the valley where Methuselah keeps his wells."

Naamah's mother frowned. "You move so often?"

"Only when wickedness grows near," Tiria said. "Noah says a place loses its blessing when men forget gratitude."

Naamah set down the jar and looked toward him again. He stood with his father, giving quiet orders, the strength in his voice unforced. When the men obeyed, it was not because they feared him, but because his faith made obedience feel like safety.

Something stirred within her then—half gratitude, half awe, and something more dangerous than either. She looked away, ashamed of the warmth that spread through her chest. He was not like the men of her village, who boasted of their own hands. This man spoke as if his strength belonged to Another.

By noon, the camp had folded like a well-practiced hand. Women walked in the center, guarded on both sides by men. Noah led at the front beside his father, eyes scanning the ridges. They moved in silence, save for the soft bleat of goats and the rustle of feet through tall grass.

As they journeyed, Naamah's mother murmured prayers of thanks. Naamah kept them in her heart but let her eyes rest often on the man who had given them reason to hope. The dew of morning had long since lifted, but its coolness remained somewhere deep inside her, where fear had once lived.

For the first time since the world had fallen to violence, she began to wonder if goodness could still prevail.

CHAPTER THREE

AMONG THE RIGHTEOUS

The valley where Noah's people dwelled was unlike any place Naamah had ever seen. The air was cool and clean, touched by the fragrance of growing things. Mist rose each morning from the earth, watering the vineyards and the fields of grain. Streams wound between groves of fig, pear, and pomegranate, their banks lined with stones smoothed by generations of careful hands.

Here, there were no walls, no idols, no altars to the false sons of heaven. Here, men labored with quiet strength, and women sang as they worked. Children laughed without fear. When the sun rose, it was met not with shouts or drunken songs, but with the low hum of prayer.

It was peace — the kind that made Naamah's chest ache.

She had never known that silence could hold so much life.

Each dawn, the camp stirred in rhythm — men to their fields, women to the flocks and looms. No command was shouted; every hand seemed to know its task as though guided by an unseen harmony. Naamah and her mother were given a tent near the gardens, shaded by an ancient olive tree whose twisted limbs had grown wide enough to shelter them both.

For days, Naamah spoke little. She listened — to the murmur of the stream, to the laughter of children, to the deep voices of men speaking blessings over the work of their hands. Her mother healed slowly, her burns fading to pale scars beneath the herbal salves. The women of the camp brought them bread, milk, and honey. No payment was asked.

"You will find it strange at first," said Tiria one morning as she kneaded dough at Naamah's side. "To live among those who still fear the Almighty. The world outside laughs at us, calls us the fools of the valley. But we are rich in what they have lost."

"What is that?" Naamah asked softly.

"Peace," Tiria said, dusting flour from her palms. "The kind that comes only from obedience."

Naamah looked across the fields to where Noah worked with his brothers. They were strengthening a small stone wall that bordered the grazing meadow. His movements were sure and deliberate, his hands roughened from labor, his tunic stained with earth. He spoke little even among his men, yet when he did, the others listened. They trusted him the way roots trust the soil — without question.

When he straightened to lift a fallen branch, she caught the light in his eyes — steady as always, but softened when he turned toward the olive grove, as though he could feel her watching. Her heart startled her with its quickened rhythm. She looked away, ashamed, and busied herself with the dough.

That evening, as the sun lowered, a gathering took place near the stream. Men and women stood in a half-circle while the elder, Lamech, spoke blessings over the day. Naamah's mother stood beside her, modestly, eyes glistening with gratitude. When the prayers ended, no one hurried away. They lingered — some laughing softly, others sitting on the grass as children climbed into their arms.

Naamah could hardly remember what laughter had sounded like before now.

Later, as she carried a jar toward the stream, she found Noah there alone, washing his hands. The evening mist rose around him, turning the air to silver. For a moment she hesitated, jar pressed against her hip. He looked up.

"You are settling well?" he asked.

"I am learning," she said. "Your people are... different."

"In what way?"

"They are kind without asking why," she said, kneeling to fill the jar. "In my village, kindness was a debt to be repaid."

He studied the water as it swirled between his fingers. "It is easier to give when you remember who gave to you first."

She considered that. "I think I am beginning to understand."

He rose, wiping his hands on the hem of his tunic. "You need not understand all at once. Even faith grows in its season."

Naamah smiled faintly, though she kept her eyes on the water. "You speak as if you tend it like a garden."

"In truth, that is all I do," he said, half-smiling. "I tend what the Almighty has given — land, beasts, family... hope. And when evil draws near, I build walls around what is good."

Her gaze lifted to meet his. "You built one around us."

For the first time, his composure wavered. "If I did, it was not I who laid the first stone." He turned his face toward the fading light. "You and your mother are safe here. But there are whispers among the men — word of the Nephilim gathering again. They will not forgive easily."

"Will you fight them?" she asked.

"I will do what is required to keep my people," he said quietly. "And to honor the One who gives them breath."

She wanted to ask more, but a voice called from across the meadow — Lamech's deep, gentle tone — and Noah inclined his head in farewell. "Do not carry water alone after dusk," he said, and left her standing by the stream, jar in hand, heart full of unspoken things.

That night, when Naamah lay beside her mother under the olive branches, she listened to the camp's quiet breathing — the murmur of life continuing in defiance of a broken world. Somewhere beyond the hills, the sons of the Watchers plotted their next cruelty. But here, for the first time since her childhood, Naamah felt safe.

And more than safe — she felt *seen*.

CHAPTER FOUR

THE
RECKONING

The sun had passed its highest place and leaned toward the west when word spread through the valley: The elders were gathering.

Men left their work in the vineyards, dusting their hands against their tunics. The younger ones went reluctantly, glancing over their shoulders at Noah, who stood by the threshing floor with his father. Even those who revered him felt the heaviness of what was coming.

By evening, a circle of stones was cleared near the stream. Mats were laid, and the older men sat first — Lamech, grey-bearded and kind-eyed; Aban, keeper of the flocks; Sethur, whose sons had been slain by the Nephilim years before; and a few from neighboring camps who had come when they heard of the rescue. The rest stood behind them in half-shadow, a wall of murmuring breath.

Women lingered at the edge of the grove, pretending to draw water or gather herbs but not fooling anyone. Naamah sat beside her mother beneath the olive tree, its roots spreading like open hands. She could not hear every word, but the tone of the voices carried clearly — deep, uncertain, rising and falling like the changing winds.

Lamech spoke first. "My son," he said quietly, "you have done a great thing, and a dangerous one. Many among us bless your courage. Yet the Nephilim are not men — their wrath burns long. Already scouts have been seen near the southern hills. If they come here, they will not only seek you. They will burn our fields, take our children. What answer do you give to that?"

Noah's voice came measured and calm. "If they come, we will defend what is ours. But I will not repent of saving the innocent. Shall we leave our neighbors to their fate because evil is strong?"

Sethur leaned forward, his hands gripping his knees. "You speak as if evil can be stopped by good intentions. I have buried sons who thought the same. We are few, Noah. Our women are few. If they are taken, our line ends. The giants care nothing for our faith."

"And if we do nothing," Noah said, "then our faith ends before our line does."

A ripple of voices followed — some agreeing, some protesting. The older men murmured of prudence, of protecting their tents, of avoiding open war. Lamech's brow furrowed, pain written in every line of his face. "Your heart is righteous," he said, "but righteousness without wisdom can destroy as swiftly as sin."

Noah rose to his feet. The movement silenced the noise. He looked around the circle, not with anger, but with a gravity that stilled even the doubters.

"When the Watchers descended," he said, "our fathers were men of strength. They knew the truth and did not bend. But fear has grown in us since then, creeping like shadow into our courage. We tell ourselves that safety is obedience, that silence is wisdom. Yet every time we bow to fear, we surrender a piece of what makes us God's people."

He paused, and the quiet that followed was so deep Naamah could hear the stream moving over stone.

"I would rather die doing what is right," he said softly, "than live long enough to forget why I was born."

From the edge of the grove, Naamah felt her heart catch. It was not pride that rang in his voice, but conviction — a strength that came from something far beyond himself.

She glanced at her mother, whose face shone in the dimming light.

Inside the circle, one of the men stood abruptly. "You speak of dying easily, Noah! You would bring death to us all."

Before Noah could answer, another voice rose — not from within the circle but from the women beyond. It was low but clear, steady despite its trembling edge.

"It was death we faced before this man came," Naamah's mother said.

All heads turned. Even Lamech straightened in surprise as she stepped forward, veiled but fearless. "You speak of danger as though it were new to us. We have seen the faces of the Nephilim. We have heard the cries of children carried off in the night. You men speak of the risk of saving others. I tell you, the greater risk is to let such evil go unchallenged."

No one moved.

She went on, voice firm. "My daughter and I are alive because of him. You call his courage reckless — I call it obedience to the Almighty who still sees and still commands justice. If there are any left in the earth who remember His name, let them be like this man."

The silence that followed was heavy, broken only by the crack of the fire. Naamah saw the struggle in many faces — shame, fear, the beginning of respect.

Lamech rose, his voice hoarse with emotion. "The matter is heard," he said finally. "Let no man speak against the rescue again. What is done was done in righteousness. May the Almighty guard our tents and guide our steps."

He placed his hand upon Noah's shoulder. For a moment father and son looked at each other — pride and worry mingling in both their eyes. Then the older men stood and dispersed quietly, speaking in low tones.

As the circle broke apart, Naamah's mother turned back toward the women. Naamah reached for her hand, but her mother's gaze lingered on Noah — who remained by the fire, unmoving. When he finally looked their way, his eyes found Naamah's in the half-light. A thousand words passed unspoken between them.

Gratitude. Respect. Something that neither dared name.

CHAPTER FIVE

THE QUIET BETWEEN WORLDS

The camp slept beneath a sky of silver. Mist rose from the ground in soft ribbons, curling around the tents and drifting upward until it disappeared into the stars. The day's arguments had faded into silence, but their weight still lingered in Noah's mind.

He sat by the last embers of the fire, turning a piece of wood in his hands. His father, Lamech, joined him slowly, his joints stiff from years of labor. The old man lowered himself beside his son without a word. For a time, they listened to the distant murmurs of the stream and the faint bleating of goats in their pen.

"You have not eaten," Lamech said at last.

"I have no hunger," Noah replied quietly.

"Because your heart is full," his father said, "and your mind cannot rest." He leaned on his staff, studying the stars that glimmered above the valley. "I remember when I was your age. The world felt vast then, and holy. Now it groans like an old beast. You hear it too, don't you?"

Noah nodded, staring into the coals. "I dreamed again last night."

Lamech's gaze sharpened. "Of what?"

"It was not like other dreams," Noah said, his voice low. "It began with silence — a silence so complete it pressed upon my chest until I could hardly breathe. Then the ground trembled beneath me, and the valleys filled with light — not fire, not water, something between the two, alive and moving. I saw mountains swallowed, yet in the midst of it there was one place that stood untouched — a plain of high ground, and upon it a shape I could not name, waiting."

Lamech's hand tightened on his staff. "Did you hear a voice?"

"No. Only the sound of the earth weeping." He looked up at his father. "Tell me, have you ever heard of such a thing?"

The old man sighed, his breath mingling with the smoke. "When I was a boy, my grandfather Methuselah told me a story handed down from his father, and from Adam himself. He said the Almighty once declared that the world, in its rebellion, would face two purgings — one by water, one by fire. He said no flesh that clings to wickedness would endure either."

Noah turned toward him. "Then it was no common dream."

"No," Lamech said softly. "Dreams such as yours are never common."He placed a hand on his son's shoulder. "Be at peace tonight. Whatever is coming, it will come in its time. You were born for days such as these — though I pray Heaven will spare you the burden it intends."

Noah lowered his head. "If such days must come, may I be found faithful."

The two men sat long in silence, the fire's glow fading to ash between them. The night around them seemed to listen.

In the women's tent, a small oil lamp burned low, its flame flickering against the woven walls. Naamah lay awake, tracing the patterns of light that danced above her. Her mother stirred beside her, then turned and smiled faintly in the dim glow.

"You have not closed your eyes all night," her mother said.

"I cannot," Naamah whispered. "My thoughts are loud."

"Loud thoughts usually have names," her mother murmured, brushing a stray curl from her daughter's face. "Will you tell me his?"

Naamah flushed, half laughing, half embarrassed. "You know already."

Her mother chuckled softly. "Ah. So it *is* the one whose courage fills every whispered story in the camp."

Naamah covered her face with her hands, smiling behind her fingers. "I know it is foolish, Mother. He is unlike any man I have known — strong, but quiet, as if the whole world speaks to him and he answers in his heart. When he looks at me, I feel as though he sees more than the dust and ashes of what I've been through... but I do not flatter myself that his thoughts ever turn toward me. Men like that do not think of such things."

Her mother tilted her head. "Men like that are still men, child. But I understand your meaning. There is a weight upon him. Some are born for ordinary joys; others carry the burdens of generations."

Naamah sighed. "Then I will not trouble my heart. I only wanted to speak it aloud — that I have noticed him... not just for what he did, but for who he is."

Her mother smiled, a glimmer of humor in her weary eyes. "Well, I have eyes too. He is not hard to look upon."

Naamah laughed softly, covering her mouth. "Mother!"

"I only speak truth," the woman said, smoothing her daughter's hair. "But remember, beauty fades, and righteousness endures. It is good you see both."

The lamp flickered lower. Outside, the wind stirred the leaves of the olive tree, whispering like a voice half-remembered. Naamah closed her eyes, her mother's hand warm against her cheek.

Somewhere not far away, Noah sat beneath the same sky, eyes lifted to the same stars. Neither knew that their hearts, in that quiet hour, had begun to move toward one another — one through faith, the other through wonder — drawn by a hand unseen.

CHAPTER SIX

THE SCOUTS
OF THE HILLS

The day began with the peace of routine. Smoke from the morning fires curled lazily upward, and the soft hum of women's voices floated through the camp as bread baked on flat stones. Naamah's hands were dusted with flour; a ring of children stood around her, giggling as she shaped the dough into small birds before setting them near the coals. Their laughter was the kind of music she had not heard since childhood — unguarded, unafraid.

Her mother, kneeling by the water jars, smiled over her shoulder. "You've found your place among them, my daughter."

"I've found my hands again," Naamah replied. "They have purpose here."

When the bread was done, she brushed the ashes from the edges and handed the warm loaves to the children. Their delight filled her chest like sunlight. She loved these small tasks — not because they were simple, but because they were *safe*. The valley, ringed with hills and fed by clear springs, felt sheltered from the violence of the world.

It was nearing midday when she saw the first sign that peace was ending.

A distant shout — sharp and hurried — carried on the wind from the eastern ridge. The laughter stilled. Men working in the fields looked up. A flock of doves, startled from the trees, lifted in a white wave and vanished into the glare.

Moments later, Noah and two of his brothers appeared on the rise above the camp, moving quickly. Dust streaked their faces. Noah's tunic was torn at the shoulder. He raised his arm in a gesture that silenced every voice.

"Gather the men," he called, his tone calm but urgent. "No one leaves the valley until we know what we face."

Naamah's heart began to pound. The women drew close together instinctively, mothers clutching their children. Her mother took her hand. "Stay by me," she whispered.

Within moments, the men of the camp assembled — strong, quiet, resolute. Noah spoke briefly to Lamech, who nodded gravely and sent two younger men running to the outlying tents. Naamah strained to hear. The only words that carried clearly were *scouts* and *markings on the stones.*

She remembered then the night of fire and terror, the roar of giants, the smoke choking her lungs. Her hand tightened on her mother's sleeve.

Noah turned to address the gathered people. "The Nephilim have not come upon us yet," he said. "But their servants have. They marked the hills with ash and bone — a warning, or a claim. We will not wait for them to return in numbers."

A murmur ran through the crowd. Some of the men reached for spears and slings. Others looked to Lamech.

Noah raised his hand again. "No panic. We act with order, not fear. We move our tents closer to the ridge of Methuselah's wells. The elders will send word to our kin there. We will not abandon this place yet, but we will be ready."

His voice was steady — not loud, but strong enough that even the frightened children stilled to listen.

Naamah watched him, her pulse quick and uncertain. The sight of him like this — commanding yet gentle, calm in the face of danger — stirred something deep within her. She remembered his hands steadying her as she ran from the burning village, the quiet power in his voice. He moved now with that same unshakable certainty.

Her mother's voice broke through her thoughts. "Do you see, Naamah? Even fear bends itself around faith in him."

"I see," Naamah said softly.

The camp shifted into motion. Women packed food, rolled mats, tied bundles. Men dismantled the smaller tents, working in pairs. The air buzzed with quiet urgency, the sound of leather cords tightening, goats bleating, children whispering questions.

Naamah and her mother worked quickly, storing the bread and covering the jars. Sweat beaded her brow, but she barely noticed. She was aware only of the heartbeat of the camp — faster now, like a drum before battle.

When she turned, Noah was suddenly there, a few paces away, speaking with one of his brothers. His arm bore a fresh scrape where the fabric had torn, the edge still red with dust. Without thinking, Naamah stepped forward.

"You are hurt," she said.

He looked at her, startled for an instant by her nearness. "It is nothing."

"Let me clean it," she said, already reaching for the cloth at her belt.

His hesitation was brief. He extended his arm. She dabbed at the scrape with water from a jar, the air between them strangely charged — quiet, close, and alive. When she looked up, their eyes met. Something passed there — recognition, perhaps, or the memory of gratitude turned into something warmer. He looked away first.

"Thank you," he said.

"You do much for others," she answered, her voice softer than she meant it to be. "Let someone tend you, at least once."

He almost smiled. "Perhaps I have."

Before she could answer, one of his brothers called his name from across the camp, and he stepped back. "Stay near the others," he said. "If you see anyone unfamiliar, sound the horn. No one wanders alone."

Naamah nodded. Her heart beat so loudly she barely heard her mother approach behind her.

"He trusts you," her mother said quietly.

Naamah turned. "He trusts everyone."

Her mother gave her a knowing look. "Not in the way he looks at you, child."

Naamah shook her head quickly, heat rushing to her cheeks. "No, Mother. He looks at all with kindness. That is his way."

Her mother smiled faintly. "Perhaps. But even the most righteous man must still see the world through human eyes."

Naamah turned away, pretending to busy herself with the bundles. Yet inside, something fragile and unfamiliar unfurled — a warmth she did not know how to name.

By dusk, the camp was half packed. Scouts were sent to watch the ridges, and fires burned low. Noah stood with Lamech and the elders, planning their movement before dawn. The air felt heavy — not yet danger, but the breath before it.

Naamah looked toward him once more before retreating into her tent. His silhouette stood tall against the fading light, a lone figure outlined in gold.

She did not know if they would face war, or flight, or another long journey into the wilderness. But she knew this:Whatever lay ahead, her heart had already chosen where it would stand.

CHAPTER SEVEN

THE MESSENGER IN THE NIGHT

The camp lay quiet beneath a low silver sky. Tents breathed in and out with sleeping bodies, and the last coals of the evening fire pressed a thin red line into the dark.

Naamah did not sleep.

She lay listening to the small sounds of night—the sigh of canvas, the soft turn of her mother on the mat, the whisper of leaves in the olive above them. The peace of the valley still held, yet something in the air felt altered, as if a hand had hovered over the world and not quite touched it.

A footstep came from the ridge. Then another, hurried but careful.

Men stirred. A shadow crossed the coals and became a man bent with travel: cloak crusted with dust, breath raw, eyes bright with urgency. He stopped at the circle of stones, lifted a hand in greeting that was also a plea.

"From Methuselah," he said, voice rasped. "I bear word for Lamech, and for Noah his son."

Within moments Lamech arrived, robe thrown over his shoulders, staff in hand. Noah followed, calm even in haste. They gave the messenger water. He drank, coughed, drank again.

"Speak," Lamech said gently.

"The lowlands smoke," the messenger answered. "Not by the hand of Heaven, but by men and the mighty ones who drive them. Fields trampled, altars defiled, wells choked with refuse. Those who once bargained for peace now pay tribute with their sons."

His eyes flicked to Noah. "Methuselah sends watchmen to every friendly ridge. He says the earth groans more loudly than ever he has heard. He says—" The man faltered, as if repeating words he did not wish to carry. "He says the Holy One will not allow this stain to deepen without answer. That the first of the old warnings is drawing near."

Lamech's fingers tightened on his staff. "The warning our fathers taught—two purgings for a faithless earth," he murmured. "One by water, one by fire."

The messenger bowed his head. "So the old man says."

Silence settled—the kind that listens.

Noah looked toward the dark line of hills, as if he could see beyond them to the wells of Methuselah and farther still to where decisions are made. His voice, when it came, was low and certain.

"Then the time of hiding ends. We will not wait to be hemmed in. At first light we move the camp toward the wells. Send word that we come with women and little ones."

"You will be received," the messenger said. "But he warns—travel guarded. Scouts swarm the crossings."

"We will travel like shepherds," Noah answered, "and leave nothing behind for jackals or giants to claim."

Lamech studied his son, sorrow and pride sharing his face. "You dreamed again," he said softly, not as a question.

Noah nodded once. "I do not yet know its name. Only its weight."

Lamech set his hand on Noah's shoulder. "The Almighty measures men before He gives them work. If He has weighed you, He has also given you strength to bear what comes."

The messenger straightened, a little steadier now that his burden was spoken. "There is one more word," he said. "For your people, but perhaps first for you."

He drew a breath, as if tasting the sentence to be sure it was whole. "Methuselah says: *Do not mistake slowness for absence. The Mercy that waits is the same Hand that judges. Prepare.*"

Noah bowed his head. "We will."

They gave the messenger bread and a resting place. Orders went out in whispers rather than shouts: coils of rope unknotted, water-skins counted, sleeping children gently turned so they might wake facing the road. The camp did not rouse fully; it leaned toward morning like a field toward light.

Lamech lingered by the coals. "My son," he said, voice almost lost in the hush, "if the first warning is near, men will think you mad before they call you faithful."

"Then let them call me mad," Noah replied, not unkindly. "I will be as I must."

They stood together a while longer, father and son sharing the warmth of small embers. At last Lamech touched Noah's cheek as he had when he was a boy and went to wake the elders.

Noah remained, alone with the thin red of the fire. He looked not fierce, but resolved—as if his soul had knelt and risen with an answer no other lips had yet spoken aloud.

Across the camp, Naamah shifted on her mat and opened her eyes to a darkness that felt newly alive. She could not hear the words that had passed, only the timbre of men's voices and the quiet that followed them. She thought of Noah's face in evening light, the steadiness of his hands, the way fear bent around faith when he spoke.

She laid her palm against the earth. It felt cool, listening.

"Something is changing," she whispered to the dark, unsure whether she meant the world or her own heart.

The olive leaves answered only with their small, sifting song. Soon, beyond the tents, a thin brightness began to gather at the farthest edge of night—morning waiting, patient as a promise.

CHAPTER EIGHT

THE JOURNEY TOWARD THE WELLS

M ist still clung to the ground when the camp began to move. The faint light before dawn turned every reed and tent rope silver. Men's voices were low, carrying orders; women moved quickly, binding baskets, tying jars, soothing sleepy children. The herd animals, sensing change, stamped and snorted against their tethers.

Naamah rose into the hush and looked around the valley that had been their refuge. Smoke rose from a few dying fires. In the dimness she could see the marks the night watchmen had left—a ring of stones broken open so no one would mistake the place for living ground again.

Her mother came beside her, wrapping a shawl around her shoulders. "Do not look back, child," she murmured. "The Lord calls us forward."

Naamah nodded but still let her eyes rest on the olive tree that had shaded their tent. It was foolish, she knew, to grieve a patch of earth. Yet each place of safety felt rarer than the one before.

A short call cut through the quiet. "Load the wagons. We move when the mist lifts." It was Noah's voice—steady, certain—and at the sound, the valley stirred like a single body waking.

The first light came as they set out. Dew gleamed on the backs of the animals; the air smelled of damp earth and crushed herbs. The line of travelers wound along the streambed toward the pass that would take them to Methuselah's wells.

Naamah and her mother walked near the center of the caravan. Children drowsed on the carts; the older boys drove the goats with switches of willow. From time to time Noah rode ahead, scanning the ridge, then doubled back with quiet words to the guards who flanked the group.

When he passed close, Naamah felt awareness follow him like heat. She kept her eyes on the path, yet always knew when he was near—the change in the rhythm of the people, the faint scent of cedar and leather as he moved by.

Her mother noticed. "You walk lighter than you did yesterday," she said softly.

Naamah smiled without answering. "It is the road. The air here is clean."

"Ah," her mother said, amused. "Then may the road stay long."

Naamah turned away to hide her grin. It was strange how even in danger her heart could lift with something almost like joy.

By midday they reached a narrow defile where rock walls rose on either side. The sun struck the cliffs, releasing the scent of stone. The men called for quiet; Noah raised his hand, and the line halted. He dismounted and studied the ground.

Lamech joined him. "Tracks?"

"Two men, perhaps three," Noah said. "They kept to the shadows, but their prints go north again. Scouts only. They did not find the camp before we left."

Lamech exhaled. "Then mercy still walks with us."

Noah nodded. "We will move on while the light is high. If they return, they will find nothing but smoke and trampled grass."

He turned, scanning the line. His gaze passed over the women, over Naamah—and paused. Only for a heartbeat, but long enough that she felt the air between them tighten. She dropped her eyes at once, her pulse unsteady.

When the line began to move again, she found herself smiling at her own foolishness. He had only been counting heads, making certain all were safe. Still, her cheeks stayed warm for a long while.

As the day wore on, the hills softened into low ridges dotted with tamarisks and flowering shrubs. Children began to laugh again; women sang under their breath to keep the rhythm of walking. The tension of departure eased slightly, though the men still watched the horizons.

Near evening they stopped by a wide meadow where a spring bubbled clear from a rock shelf. The camp re-formed with practiced order: tents rising like petals, fires coaxed from tinder, animals penned in rope circles. When her work was done, Naamah carried a jar to the spring.

She found Noah there already, rinsing dust from his arms. The water caught the gold of the setting sun and threw it back against his skin. He looked up as she approached, and for a moment neither spoke.

"You lead us well," she said finally.

He shook his head. "The road was merciful today. That is not my doing."

"Still," she said, "it takes a steady hand to keep fear behind and hope ahead."

He studied her a moment, then smiled—briefly, almost reluctantly. "You have a gift for speaking plainly."

"I was raised among people who hid truth," she said. "It seems a waste of breath."

The smile deepened, then faded as he looked toward the darkening horizon. "The world is changing faster than we can walk. Every valley we leave behind feels heavier."

Naamah dipped her jar into the spring. "Then perhaps this one will lighten it again."

He looked at her then—not as commander or savior, but simply as a man seeing another soul who understood. The air seemed to still between them. She lowered her gaze quickly and rose.

"I should take this to my mother," she said.

He inclined his head. "Rest well, Naamah."

Her name in his voice felt like both blessing and warning. She carried the jar carefully, afraid her trembling hands might spill its contents.

That night, the camp slept ringed by torches. Lamech and Noah kept watch with a few of the younger men. The hills lay quiet, but somewhere far off, a single wolf gave its low cry to the darkness.

In the women's tent, Naamah lay awake, eyes tracing the flicker of light through the woven walls. Her mother slept beside her, peaceful. Outside, she heard Noah's voice—low, giving quiet orders—and knew she would carry that sound with her into sleep.

The journey had begun, and though she did not yet know its end, her heart had already set its course.

CHAPTER NINE

SIGNS ON THE WIND

B y the third day the air grew heavy and still. The mist that usually rose at dawn did not come; instead, a pale haze clung low to the earth as if the ground itself were holding its breath. The travelers felt it in their bones—a strangeness in the wind that moved without sound, stirring the hair on their arms but not the leaves of the trees.

Naamah walked beside one of the wagons, helping a small boy steady a jar. The child pointed upward. "Why does the sky look like that?"

She followed his finger. The blue had deepened to a dull gray-green, and the light of morning came as if through polished bronze. "It is only dust from the far valleys," she told him gently, though the lie tasted strange on her tongue.

Noah rode near the front of the caravan. Every few moments he paused, scanning the ridges, his eyes narrowing against the glare. Lamech followed on foot, leaning on his staff but keeping pace with surprising strength. Around them the hills grew steeper, carved by narrow paths that twisted between stands of thorn and wild fig.

By noon they came to a plateau where the stream they had been following vanished underground. Noah called a halt. "We rest here," he said. "The scouts will go ahead to find the next spring."

The men obeyed, grateful for shade. Women spread cloths and passed bread, but few spoke. Even the children played quietly, their laughter subdued by the strange weight in the air.

Naamah sat with her mother beneath a cluster of tamarisks. The branches whispered faintly, their thin leaves catching what little breeze there was. "Something is near," her mother said softly. "Do you feel it?"

Naamah nodded. "It feels like waiting."

A shout broke the quiet. One of the young men came running from the northern ridge, breathless. "Noah!"

Noah rose at once. "What is it?"

The scout pointed behind him, gasping. "Smoke—from the valley we left. A column rising high. And...the stones—the markings—more of them. They burned the olive grove."

A murmur spread through the camp like wind through dry grass. The women clutched their children; the men reached instinctively for weapons that would be useless against giants.

Noah's face remained calm, though his jaw tightened. "They found the valley," he said quietly to Lamech. "They are claiming what we left."

Lamech's eyes closed briefly. "Then we were right to move."

"Yes," Noah said, "but it will not end there." He turned to the men. "We move again before sunset. The wells of Methuselah are a day's walk east. We must reach them before full dark."

He moved among the people, giving instructions—firm, gentle, practical. His presence steadied them. Naamah watched him from a distance, admiring how his calm spread through the camp like water through sand.

Her mother followed her gaze. "I see the hand of the Almighty on him, don't you?"

Naamah nodded. "Yes... and yet he seems burdened by it."

"Such men always are," her mother said. "They carry the weight of things not yet seen."

Naamah's eyes lingered on Noah a moment longer before she turned to help pack their tent.

They traveled hard that afternoon. The sun dipped low, and the land opened into a long valley cut by shallow streams. On the far side, the first of Methuselah's wells gleamed in the fading light.

Cries of relief rippled through the caravan. The old man himself stood waiting at the edge of the settlement—tall, stooped, his white beard catching the last gold of the sun. Behind him, a circle of men with staffs and slings formed a living gate.

"Noah, son of Lamech," Methuselah said as they approached, his voice deep and cracked with age. "You have come in wisdom. The air itself bears warning."

"We saw the smoke," Noah said. "The Nephilim claim our valley."

Methuselah's eyes narrowed. "Then the corruption spreads faster than I feared. You will rest here tonight, but you must not linger. The cities below have grown bold; they send scouts to take what is pure."

Noah bowed his head. "We will obey your counsel."

The old man laid a hand on his shoulder. "You have dreamed, I know it. I can see it in your eyes. Do not speak it yet. The hour is not come—but it will."

Naamah stood with her mother at the rear of the line, watching the meeting. She felt awe stir in her chest. The sight of the two men—ancient Methuselah, the last living link to Adam, and Noah, young yet carrying the same gravity—filled her with both fear and wonder.

When Methuselah's gaze drifted toward the people, it paused on her. His eyes, clouded though they were, seemed to pierce straight through the crowd and rest on her face. He smiled faintly. "There are purposes woven long before we understand them," he murmured, as if to himself.

Naamah looked down quickly, uncertain why her heart had leapt.

That night the camp settled by the wells. The water was cool and sweet, and the children laughed again. For the first time in days, some hope returned. But as Naamah lay beneath the open sky, she could not shake the feeling that the world was shifting beneath them.

Far away, lightning flickered on the horizon—soundless, distant, like the heartbeat of a sleeping giant.

And Noah, standing watch near the wells, felt the same tremor pass through his spirit. He looked toward the unseen cities beyond the hills and whispered a prayer he did not understand:

"Lord, make me ready."

CHAPTER TEN

AT THE WELLS OF THE ANCIENTS

T he wells lay like polished eyes in the earth, circled with stones smoothed by a thousand faithful hands. Willows ringed the water with a fine green canopy, and carved markers—older than any living man—kept watch from the ridges. It was a place that felt held, as if the ground itself remembered who had first called the Holy One by name.

Methuselah stood at the foremost spring with a staff of olive wood, the bark worn to silk where his palm had rested through the years. He was tall still, though the weight of days had bowed him; his hair fell like winter's light to his breast, and his eyes—clouded yet keen—missed little. When Noah drew near, the old man's mouth softened into something like a smile.

"Grandson of Lamech," he said, voice warm as bread, "you arrive with more lives than you left with. This is how a man should travel."

Noah bowed. "Grandfather, we bring gratitude and work, not burdens."

"Gratitude and work," Methuselah echoed, amused. "Two strong ropes that hold a world together."

He turned his face to the people—women stooping to fill jars, children clutching the hems of garments, men easing beasts to water. "You are welcome in this circle," he told them. "No hand raised against you will prosper—not while I live."

The words moved through the camp like a blessing, easing backs and loosening breath. Even the guards at the well's edge let their shoulders drop by a finger's width.

Naamah stood with her mother among the women, jar against her hip. She had expected awe; she had not expected the gentleness that sat on the old man like a cloak. When Methuselah's gaze turned, it paused upon her—not piercing, not heavy, only seeing. He made a small motion, and she stepped nearer before she realized she had moved.

"You are new to our circle," Methuselah said, studying her as one studies a flower he once knew by another name.

"Yes, my lord," Naamah answered, eyes lowered. "I am Naamah, daughter of Tirzah."

"Tirzah," he repeated, nodding toward her mother with recognition. "Your father traded goats at the southern fairs before men there forgot to bless the giver of goats." His eyes returned to Naamah. "You carry questions the way other girls carry bracelets."

Heat rose to her cheeks. "If questions are too many, I can put them down."

He chuckled—an old creek finding its voice. "Keep them. Questions are buckets; they draw truth from deep places."

Naamah's mother inclined her head. "My daughter honors wisdom."

"And wisdom will honor her," Methuselah said simply. He lifted a hand, palm outward—a gesture of welcome—and moved on to lay that same gentle blessing upon others.

Noah watched the exchange from a respectful distance. The old man's kindness was not new to him, but the ease with which Methuselah received Naamah kindled a quiet warmth in Noah's chest. He pushed the thought aside and went to his work, setting men to mend a crumbled well-wall and posting watchers along the northern ridge.

By afternoon the camp had found its rhythm. Ropes were retwined; bread rose under cloths; a circle of boys learned the sling from a patient elder. The land itself seemed to breathe more evenly.

Near the oldest well—lined with stones bearing faint, ancient marks—Methuselah sat beneath a woven shade. Naamah, carrying two small jars, slowed as she passed. The old man patted the reed mat beside him.

"Sit," he said. "Let an old tree rest in company."

She set the jars carefully and folded herself onto the mat. Up close she could see the fine network of lines fanning from his eyes, as if laughter and sorrow had taken equal turns there. A carved tablet lay on his lap, smoothed by generations of fingers. The symbols were simple, elegant.

"What is written?" she asked softly.

"Names," he said. "Those who called upon the Creator when the world was young. I touch them when I forget who we are."

Naamah traced a letter in the air. "Did you know Adam?"

"Through those who did, but my eyes have seen him" Methuselah answered, gaze far and near at once. "I learned the sound of his grief and the taste of his hope. He taught our fathers how to remember—stone and word and the setting of a table. The earth was different then." He tipped his head, listening to something beyond the well's gurgle. "Clearer. As if everything agreed with everything else."

"And now?" Naamah asked, though her heart half-feared the answer.

"Now everything argues," he said. "Even the ground quarrels with the foot that treads it. But do not mistake confusion for victory. Corruption shouts; faith endures."

Naamah gathered courage. "I have heard that even the sons of heaven—those who fell—do not touch you."

He did not smile at that. He grew grave. "They remember what they once were, and what they once vowed. Some vows stain. Some protect. The Holy One has set a hedge around me until He says otherwise."

"Are you—" She hesitated, searching. "Afraid?"

"Of them? No." His eyes warmed. "Of forgetting? Yes. That is why we keep wells and stories."

They sat in companionable quiet. Across the clearing Noah's voice rose and fell, giving quiet orders; the men lifted stones and settled them true. Naamah found her gaze drifting without permission.

"You favor him," Methuselah said, as if noting a change in weather.

"I—" She bent quickly to fuss with the jar straps. "He saved us. My favor is gratitude."

"Gratitude is the seed of many things," the old man said mildly. "It grows into loyalty, sometimes into love. Sometimes into a will that will not break when all else does."

Naamah kept her eyes down. "He is a great tree. I am a reed."

"Then you have not watched reeds in a flood," Methuselah murmured, and Naamah glanced up, puzzled by a word she did not yet understand in the old man's mouth.

"Forgive me," he said gently. "An old tongue trips over itself. I mean only that strength has many shapes."

He shifted the tablet on his knee. "Walk with me, child."

He rose, steadied by her hand and his staff, and she followed him along the circle of stones. He touched a notch here, a groove there, fingers mapping memory. "Our fathers marked the world to remember where Heaven had met earth," he said. "A well. An altar. A marriage. Each a promise renewed."

They came upon a small standing stone half-sunk in soil, its face carved with a simple braid. Methuselah brushed the dust from the braid with tender care. "This," he said, "was placed when my mother took my father's hand. He told me he felt the world steady under his feet that day."

Naamah smiled, shy. "That is a strong feeling."

"Strong enough to bear a calling," he said. His eyes, clouded but true, shifted toward where Noah labored. "A man holds fast when he is held fast. Remember that."

Naamah's breath caught. "You speak as if you see the end of a road you have not yet walked."

"I see only as much as a hedge lets me," he said, amused at himself again. "Enough to bless a beginning when the Maker brings it near."

He took her hand then—lightly, grandfather-soft—and set it upon the cool stone. "Curiosity is not hunger without manners," he said. "It is the mind's gratitude. Ask, learn, keep. You will be needed for what is to come."

"What is to come?" she asked, barely more than breath.

He released her hand. "Work. Much work. And mercy, if we ask for it."

Toward evening a murmuring ran along the ridge watchers and down through the camp: riders—or what passed for riders in those days—moving along the far hills, not drawing near, only noting. Noah went to the lookout, stood long with a palm braced on the stone. When he returned, his face was untroubled but set.

"We double the outer guard at night," he told Lamech. "No fires on the rim. Children sleep near the wells."

Lamech grunted approval. "They circle like vultures who mistake living men for carrion."

"They will learn their mistake," Noah said quietly.

Before the light failed, Methuselah called the people to the water. He spoke without staff or flourish, as a father at his own table.

"Give thanks," he said simply. "Not because our enemies sleep, but because the Giver does not."

They lifted their voices—not loudly, not with practiced song, but with the plain, warm sound of a people who still remembered whom to thank. Naamah's throat tightened; her mother's fingers found hers and squeezed.

Afterward, as families turned to their tents, Naamah carried a jar toward the elder's shade once more. Noah was already there, standing respectful as a younger oak before an older one. Methuselah looked between them with a satisfaction he did not bother to hide.

"I have two ears," he said lightly. "One for counsel, one for stories. Which will you fill first?"

"Counsel," Noah said at once.

"Stories," Naamah said at the same time, then flushed. Methuselah laughed, delighted.

"Then we are rich," he said. "Counsel keeps us alive; stories remind us why."

He gestured for them to sit, and—after the smallest flicker of hesitation—they did, not touching, not even close, but held in the same small circle of evening. The elder spoke of first orchards and honest weights, of how men once sang while building and rested when the land did. He spoke, too,—soberly—of the Watchers, and the moment when their beauty curdled to hunger.

"I was a boy when the first of their sons came north," he said. "We did not yet know how to name their appetites. But the ground knew. It drank more blood in one season than it had in a hundred years."

Noah's jaw hardened. Naamah's hands tightened around the jar strap.

Methuselah laid his palm flat upon the earth. "There is an old saying my father kept: *When the ground is forced to drink what is not its wine, it calls for a new vintage.*" His eyes found Noah's, then Naamah's. "I think the ground has been calling a long time."

He let the words settle, not forcing them to go farther than they wished.

When the first stars pricked the deepening blue, Methuselah rose. "Enough for one evening," he said. "To-morrow there will be fences to mend and lines to teach the boys. And if the Holy One is kind, bread enough to share twice."

He touched Noah's shoulder in passing—blessing more than affection—then reached for Naamah's hand. "Walk steady, child," he murmured, pressing the faintest weight of the carved tablet against her fingers before taking it back. "Buckets, remember."

As he went, Noah and Naamah found themselves for the smallest moment alone within the hum of settling tents. They did not speak. But the old man's stories lay between them like laid stones, marking a path neither had yet named.

From the far ridge came the thin call of a watcher's horn—their watcher, not ours. The camp answered with its own low note: present, unafraid.

Naamah lifted her jar. "Good night," she said, and the words felt larger than ordinary.

"Good night," Noah answered, and in his voice lay counsel and story, duty and—though neither would have dared say it—hope.

CHAPTER ELEVEN

THE LESSONS AND THE VISITOR

Morning broke soft and golden over the wells. A light mist floated across the stones, curling around the feet of those who gathered to hear Methuselah speak. He sat on a low rock near the oldest spring, his hands resting on the staff carved by his father — before silence had come between men and their Maker.

Noah stood close, attentive, his eyes steady. Naamah lingered behind a circle of women, her arms wrapped around her knees, pretending to tie a rope so she might listen without seeming bold.

"The world was young," Methuselah began, "when the first altar smoked upon the earth. There were no idols then — only stones lifted by willing hands. Blood was shed, yes, but not to appease. It was to remember."He looked up at the faces around him. "The Almighty does not hunger as we do. He desires honor, not meat. He listens for hearts turned toward Him. And to those who listen, He still speaks."

The people were silent. Only the sound of water murmuring over stone answered him.

"Some hear Him in dreams," Methuselah said softly. "Some through messengers who bear the glow of Heaven. Once, He walked among us — and man trembled but lived. Do not think those days are ended. The Eternal has not lost His voice. It is men who have stopped their ears."

He turned his gaze to Noah. "To honor is to obey. To obey is to remember Who we serve."

Noah bowed his head. "And if His voice is hard to discern?"

"Then quiet the heart," Methuselah said. "He will not shout over the noise of fear."

The crowd nodded thoughtfully. A breeze moved across the wells, stirring the fringe of Naamah's shawl. A jar slipped from a child's grasp and shattered against the stones, startling the group. Naamah bent to gather the shards — and Noah was suddenly there, crouching beside her, his hand brushing hers as they reached for the same piece.

Their eyes met briefly — a flicker of surprise, a warmth neither understood. She looked away, cheeks flushed, and Noah rose, giving her the smallest nod before stepping back into the circle.

Methuselah smiled faintly, as if he had seen the whole exchange without looking. "Let every hand mend what it breaks," he said, eyes glinting with gentle humor. "And every heart learn to listen before it speaks."

The lesson ended in laughter — light, cleansing, human. By midday, the camp had returned to its rhythm: men strengthening the outer walls, women baking bread, children carrying water skins. Nothing in the sky hinted that the day would end differently than it began.

Evening came softly, the sun orange against the ridge. Smoke from cooking fires rose straight into the still air. The world, for a moment, seemed perfectly at rest.

Then the quiet deepened — not suddenly, but like a breath held too long. The laughter faded, the goats stilled, and the wind forgot its path. The silence was not empty; it was *watching*.

Naamah felt it first — the tiny hairs along her arms prickling. She turned toward the far end of camp where the wells caught the last light. A few of the men had stopped their work. Children were gathered up, held close. No alarm, no shout — only instinct, the kind that was deeper than words.

And then he was there.

No sound of approach, no shadow across the ridge — simply presence, as if the space beyond the wells had decided to take form.

He was tall, but not giant; graceful, but not human. The air around him shimmered faintly, like heat over a forge. His face was neither young nor old, and beauty clung to him like light to polished bronze. Yet there was something unbearable in it — a perfection so severe it ached to look upon. His eyes were the color of metal quenched in water, and when he spoke, his voice carried the depth of distant thunder.

"Methuselah."

The name rang across the camp. People flinched but did not fall; none bowed. Mothers covered their children's faces; men stepped back, weapons raised by instinct rather than hope.

Methuselah rose slowly, his staff firm in his hand. His expression was calm, almost welcoming. "You were not summoned," he said, his voice carrying like a bell through the silence.

"Nor forbidden," the being replied. "I come under peace."

"You come under guilt," Methuselah answered evenly.

A faint smile touched the Watcher's lips — not amusement, but acknowledgment. "I come to look upon the one the Almighty still calls favored. There are few of your kind left who remember the sound of His voice."

"And fewer still of yours who regret losing it," Methuselah said.

The Watcher's gaze shifted toward the people — not unkindly, but curious, almost wistful. "They fear me."

"They remember what your kind brought upon them."

A silence fell again. The Watcher stepped closer — but his foot stopped just short of the stone ring that encircled the wells. His eyes flickered downward. Though invisible, something vast and unseen pressed against him. The air between him and Methuselah quivered like water against a glass.

He could not cross.

For the first time, his expression changed — not anger, but something close to pain. "You are still guarded."

Methuselah inclined his head. "Not by my strength. By His mercy."

The Watcher's voice softened. "You have lived long, elder. You have seen the rise and fall of faith. Tell me — do you not tire of being forgotten? The Almighty you serve is slow to answer, even slower to defend."

"The slow river still reaches the sea," Methuselah said.

A faint tremor of emotion rippled through the Watcher's perfect features. "You believe judgment will save this world."

"I believe obedience will save the obedient," Methuselah said simply.

For a long moment, neither moved. It felt to those watching as though the entire camp was suspended between two eternities — one of light, one of shadow — both held in the hands of ancient beings who had outlived the memory of mountains.

Finally, the Watcher lowered his gaze. When he spoke again, his voice was quiet, almost weary. "Soon the Holy will speak again. When He does, the earth will tremble, and men will hide from His words. You will not live to see it, Methuselah — but your blood will. And he will be tested beyond measure."

His eyes turned briefly toward Noah, who stood motionless beside Lamech.

Methuselah's face softened, though his voice remained steady. "Then may that test refine him."

The Watcher inclined his head in respect — a small gesture that seemed enormous in that stillness. "When mercy ends," he said, "even mountains will learn to weep."

And without sound or wind, he was gone.

The air returned all at once — the chirr of insects, the crackle of fires, the whimper of a child who did not know why he cried. The people drew breath again.

Methuselah stood unmoving, eyes on the place where the Watcher had been. After a moment, he turned to the camp. "Fear not," he said. "He was not given leave to harm us."

Then, lowering his gaze to Noah, he added quietly, "But we are not given leave to slumber, either."

Naamah pressed a hand against her heart, the beat wild beneath her palm. She looked at Noah — his face pale in the firelight, eyes fixed on Methuselah with a mix of awe and determination. She knew, without knowing why, that nothing in their world would ever again be the same.

CHAPTER TWELVE

ECHOES OF THE VISITOR

N o one truly slept that night.

Fires burned low, not for warmth but for courage. From tent to tent voices rose and fell in hushed argument—the same questions circling like moths around flame.

"Was it truly one of the Watchers?" "Why did he come here?" "What did Methuselah mean when he said we cannot slumber?"

The elders offered calm answers, but even calm sounded brittle. Mothers held their children close, whispering prayers half-remembered from their own mothers. The men kept their spears near, though all knew such wood would be nothing against the being they had seen.

Naamah lay awake beside her mother, staring at the faint glow that seeped through the tent wall. Every time she closed her eyes, she saw again the perfect stillness of that figure—the beauty so sharp it had cut the breath from her chest. She shivered, not from fear of him, but from the weight of what his presence meant.

Her mother spoke into the darkness. "You saw him clearly?"

"Yes," Naamah whispered.

"Describe him."

Naamah hesitated. "He was...terrible, but not ugly. Like a flame that knows it can burn anything and still chooses not to."

Her mother was quiet for a long moment. "Your father used to say the fallen were like that—half light, half pride. We were warned never to envy their glory."

"I did not envy him," Naamah said softly. "But I pitied him. He looked...lonely."

Her mother reached for her hand. "Then you saw truly."

Outside, a goat bleated once and fell silent. Somewhere a man coughed, the sound small against the endless dark. When Naamah finally drifted toward sleep, she dreamed of eyes like molten metal watching the world from afar.

By dawn, the camp was stirring again—slow, subdued, as if every sound might wake something best left sleeping.

The smell of bread and smoke mingled with the hush of unease.

Noah found Methuselah seated by the wells, staff across his knees, face turned to the sun that had just cleared the ridge. The elder looked tired but peaceful, like a man who had spent the night speaking with unseen company.

Noah approached and waited until Methuselah opened his eyes.

"Was he what I think he was?" Noah asked.

"Yes," Methuselah said simply.

"Why come now?"

"To remember what reverence feels like," the old man answered. "Even the fallen crave the warmth they cast away."

Noah frowned. "He said I would be tested."

"And so you will," Methuselah said. "Every man is tested, but some are tested for the sake of many."

"Is that why the Almighty still speaks to you?" Noah asked quietly. "Because you listen?"

The old man's smile was faint. "Because I answer. Listening without obedience is only curiosity."

They sat together for a while. "Do not let fear make you deaf," Methuselah said at last. "The Holy One will speak again—perhaps to you. When He does, remember what you saw last night. Power is loud. Truth is quiet."

Noah bowed his head. "Then I will learn to hear quiet things."

Methuselah placed a hand on his shoulder. "That is the beginning of wisdom."

Across the camp, Naamah and her mother were kneading dough near the fire. The other women worked silently until Tirzah spoke in a low voice. "My daughter thinks too much. She will burn the bread."

Naamah smiled faintly. "My thoughts are full. The world feels larger today."

Her mother's hands paused in the dough. "Larger, or emptier?"

"I'm not sure," Naamah admitted. "When I saw the Watcher, I was afraid—but when I saw Noah stand beside Methuselah, I felt something else. Safe, maybe. As if goodness still has weight enough to stand against such things."

Tirzah regarded her a moment, then nodded. "It does. But remember—men who carry that kind of goodness often walk hard roads. If your heart ever binds itself to such a man, it will have to be strong."

Naamah looked down, dusting flour from her palms. "Then perhaps I should begin strengthening it now."

Her mother laughed softly, but there was sadness in the sound. "You always were your father's child.

That evening, the camp grew quiet again, but not from fear—more like reverence. Men repaired fences; women hummed songs older than memory. Children played at guarding the wells, waving sticks as if defending the world.

Naamah went to draw water. Noah was already there, binding a new rope to the bucket. They greeted each other with a small nod, unsure what to say. The silence between them was not awkward; it felt sacred.

"Did you sleep?" he asked finally.

"Barely," she admitted. "I kept seeing his face."

"I saw something else," Noah said. "Methuselah's calm. He didn't flinch. It was as if the earth itself trusted him."

Naamah tilted her head. "You're not afraid anymore."

"I'm still afraid," he said. "But fear no longer tells me what to do."

They both watched the bucket sink, the rope whispering through Noah's hands. When he drew it up and handed it to her, their fingers brushed. For a moment, the world seemed to steady—two small lives anchored against something vast.

Naamah smiled. "Then perhaps the Almighty has already begun to speak."

Noah's eyes met hers. "Perhaps He speaks through many things."

She carried the jar back to camp, heart pounding for reasons she could not name. Behind her, Noah looked toward the horizon where the last light faded and thought he heard the faintest echo of a voice carried on the wind—gentle, commanding, alive.

CHAPTER THIRTEEN

THE DAYS OF QUIET GROWTH

T hree weeks passed, and the wells found their rhythm again. Each morning the camp woke to the creak of ropes, the thud of wooden buckets, the splash of water poured into waiting jars. By midmorning, the air shimmered with heat and the smell of baked bread; by nightfall, the fires ringed the clearing like small suns, each circle of light wrapped in laughter and song.

Children played their new favorite game—guarding the wells from "giants"—while mothers pretended not to see the bent sticks they used for spears. Their small shouts of victory carried across the valley, a sound the elders said made even the stones feel younger, referring to themselves.

Naamah and her mother worked each day beside the women who spun flax and prepared herbs. Her hands, once trembling from fear, had grown strong again. She smiled more easily now, though she still started at sudden noises. Sometimes, while drawing water, she caught herself humming—bits of the old melodies Methuselah taught the camp, songs meant to keep the heart turned upward.

Noah spent most days repairing fences, teaching younger men to strengthen the walls with living vines instead of dead branches. At night he joined Methuselah to record measures of time, and names, the old man dictating while Noah scratched the words into damp clay. The younger men watched him with quiet respect, though they rarely understood what he and the elder discussed so late by the fire.

One evening, Methuselah leaned closer over the tablet. "Every generation leaves a mark, Noah," he said. "But few know what they are writing until the clay is dry."

"I want mine to be faithful," Noah answered.

The old man's eyes glinted. "Then keep listening. The Holy One speaks still—but not always in thunder. Sometimes He waits behind silence until a heart is quiet enough to hear."

Noah nodded, but the words left a weight on his chest that felt like both promise and burden.

Naamah often watched them from the shadows of the women's tents, fascinated by how easily the two men understood one another—one so young, one older than memory. She admired Noah's patience, his gentleness with those slower to learn. Sometimes she wished she could thank him again for what he had done months before, yet gratitude had changed shape inside her; it had become something warmer, something harder to speak.

One night, as the camp settled, she found herself walking toward the outer fence where Noah worked by torchlight, fitting new vines along the posts. She hesitated at the edge of the glow. "You never rest," she said quietly.

He looked up, surprised but not displeased. "The vines grow while we sleep. I'm only giving them guidance."

"Even vines need rest," she teased, then bit her lip. "Forgive me—I forget my place."

He shook his head. "You forget nothing. You speak truth." He stepped aside, gesturing to the woven wall. "Come see. The living stems will hold longer than cut wood. The roots keep feeding what protects us."

She ran her fingers lightly over the green weave. "It's beautiful," she said. "Alive and protecting—like the Almighty's hand."

Noah smiled. "That was Methuselah's thought, not mine. He says every wall should breathe, else it becomes a prison."

Naamah looked up at him, the torchlight soft on his face. "You listen well."

"Sometimes," he said. "Other times I only try."

Their eyes held, and for a moment the distance between duty and longing narrowed to a breath. Then a shout from across the camp broke the spell—one of the boys calling that supper was ready. Noah stepped back, the polite half-bow of a man reminding himself of boundaries.

"Good night, Naamah."

She lowered her head, smiling. "Good night, Noah."

Later that night, as she and her mother spread their blankets, Tirzah spoke drowsily. "You're quiet again."

"Just thinking," Naamah said.

"About the vines?" her mother teased.

"Perhaps."

Tirzah chuckled, turning on her side. "Then think kindly, but remember—men like Noah are called to things larger than tents and gardens. Loving such a man is not a small work."

Naamah smiled into the dim light. "No, I imagine it isn't," she said softly. Then, after a beat, she added with a shy laugh, "But it might be easier when the man happens to be as handsome as he is."

Her mother laughed outright, the sound muffled by the blanket she pulled over her shoulder. "Ah, so the truth appears at last."

Naamah grinned, cheeks warm. "I'm only saying the Almighty gives beauty where He knows it will be noticed."

Tirzah's laughter faded into a sigh. "Then may you notice wisely, my daughter."

Naamah watched the embers fading through the open flap and whispered, half to herself, "I'll try."

Chapter Fourteen

THE WEDDING FEAST

The wells wore garlands.

River reeds braided with wildflowers hung from the standing stones; shells polished to a soft gleam cupped tiny flames along the pathways. Bread rose under cloths perfumed with mint, and pots of honeyed figs cooled in the evening shade. Laughter threaded the camp from tent to tent as women sang happy songs and men carried benches to the clearing.

Naamah stood with a ring of young women beneath a shady tree, fingers quick as birds while they wove a crown for the bride. Tiria's daughter, Sela, leaned her shoulder to Naamah's with a conspirator's grin.

"Do not make it too fine," Sela teased. "If the bride looks like a queen, her husband will forget to breathe."

"He will remember when she tells him," another girl laughed, and the circle burst into easy giggles. They were kind to Naamah, drawing her into their warmth.

Naamah smiled, threading a blue-stemmed blossom into place. "If a crown can enchant a husband, I will weave a beautiful one".

"Listen!" Sela lifted her chin. Across the clearing, the groom's friends tested a drum; a thin reed flute chased the rhythm with a bright, nimble tune. "They will dance before the stars wake."

"They will dance until the stars sleep," said an older woman fondly, passing with a tray. "Hurry—bring the garlands."

They went laughing into the open, arms full of blossoms and greenery. The bride—Methuselah's granddaughter, Miryam—waited near the oldest well with her mother, hair braided with a simple ribbon, joy lighting her face. The groom, Elior, stood under the shade with his father, each man trying and failing not to grin.

When the people had gathered, Methuselah lifted his hand. The murmurs fell like leaves.

He did not stand high or raise his voice. He simply turned so his face held the morning and the bride and groom at once, and spoke as a father who had blessed a hundred harvests.

"Two hands," he said gently, "are given to build what the Almighty keeps. These hands"—he looked from Miryam to Elior—"have learned to work and to bless, may they learn to rejoice. The Holy One gives union not as a wall against sorrow, but as a lamp within it."

He touched their joined fingers with his staff, an old, tender gesture. "Walk in honor. Listen when Heaven speaks. And may your laughter be a sign in a darkening age."

"Amen," the elders breathed, and the camp echoed them.

The couple turned to one another, shy and blazing, and the flute leapt—quick as birds over water. Music spilled through the clearing; the drum took the heartbeat and made it bright. Women clapped time, men stamped the dust in patterns their fathers had stamped, and the first dance—circles within circles—swept them all like a warm, clean wind.

Naamah let herself be pulled in. Sela caught her hand; another girl caught the other; the ring widened and narrowed with laughter. The rhythm found her feet before her thoughts could. For a moment she forgot the fire of her old village and the chill of the Watcher's eyes; the world was only light and dust and the mercy of breath.

When the circle broke for partners, a young man stepped forward and bowed with good-natured flourish. "Naamah, daughter of Tirzah—dance with me?"

He was Eiran, the flax-worker's son—broad-shouldered, sun-browned, eyes bright with kindness. She glanced across the clearing without meaning to. Noah stood with Lamech near the row of lamps, smiling as he spoke to one of the elders. He did not see her.

Naamah offered Eiran her hand. "Gladly."

They turned with the drum. He had an easy step and a voice that tripped over jokes faster than he could finish them.

"You are too solemn for a girl who smiles like sunlight," he said, half-teasing, half-true.

"I have been learning to remember how," she answered, breathless.

"Then remember tonight," he grinned. "No giants, no scouts, only bread and song."

They spun; the flute climbed; girls' bracelets chimed like little bells. When the set ended, Eiran led her back to the circle with a courteous bow. "If your feet forgive me later, I will ask again," he said, and went to sweep his laughing mother into a dance.

Across the firelight, Noah's smile had softened to something quieter. He watched the bride and groom whirl, then—against his own instruction—let his gaze find Naamah. She stood flushed and laughing, one palm pressed to her ribs as if to keep her heart from leaping out. Joy suited her; it made her look like she belonged to it.

"You are thinking too hard for a feast," Methuselah murmured at his side.

"I am considering the needs of the watch," Noah said, too quickly.

"Ah." Methuselah's eyes glinted. "And the watch has honey on its hands?"

Noah exhaled, almost a chuckle, almost a sigh. "She should dance with men who make her laugh. My life is...not light."

"Light is not weighed by laughter alone," the old man said. "When your heart finds stillness in another's joy, it is listening." He spared Noah further rescue by tapping his staff toward the clearing. "Go, make certain the children do not spill the lamps. It will ease your mind."

Noah obeyed—grateful, chastened, still smiling.

As dusk deepened, the feast lengthened into stories. Elders told of clean harvests and early marriages; women added the truth of how such stories had actually gone. Children clambered onto benches to see. Someone passed a platter toward Naamah and Sela; someone else slipped garlands over Lamech's shoulders to general cheering.

Eiran reappeared at Naamah's elbow with two cups of watered wine. "For courage," he said lightly, "in case another dance finds you."

"My feet are braver than my tongue," she confessed, taking a sip.

"Then I shall ask your feet," he said, and they both laughed.

"Go with him!" Sela hissed, delighted. "Or I will steal him myself."

"I would like to see you try," Eiran said, and made them both laugh again.

When the music surged anew, Naamah did not resist. She let Eiran lead her back into the ring. But mid-turn, a ripple of quiet moved through her—not alarm, not sorrow, only the sudden awareness of a steady presence at the edge of the light. She looked up. Noah had lifted a toddler from the dust, drying the child's tears with the edge of his sleeve. He spoke a word she could not hear; the child hiccuped and broke into a grin. The moment was small, ordinary, and it cut through her like a sweet ache.

"Are you well?" Eiran asked, keeping the step.

"Yes," she said, finding her smile again. "Very."

When the tunes grew slower and the lamps threw softer circles, Naamah slipped away for air. The wells gleamed dark as sky. She walked to the nearest stone and set her fingers against its cool face, feeling the hum of the day settle inside her.

Footsteps paused behind her. "The bride says the garlands did not make the groom forget to breathe," Noah said, voice easy.

Naamah turned, amused. "Then our work failed."

"Or succeeded," he said. "The Almighty prefers husbands who breathe."

They stood a respectful pace apart. Even the quiet between them felt watched over.

"You were kind with the children," she said.

"They are easier than fences," he said. "They come mended by morning."

She smiled, then looked toward the dance. "It is a good night."

"It is," he said. "I am glad you danced."

"With a friend," she said quickly, an unnecessary shield.

"With a friend," he agreed. He did not add what sat unspoken on his tongue: that joy looked right upon her, that his peace had lengthened each time he caught the sound of her laugh. Instead he nodded toward the lights. "They will sing until the stars complain."

She breathed a small laugh. "Then the stars must learn patience."

They both turned at the same moment—she toward Sela's waving arms, he toward a boy calling his name near the goat pens. For an instant they held each other's gaze, steady and unafraid, and then the moment passed as gently as it had come.

Naamah rejoined the women, who were already gossiping softly about the bride's veil, the sweet figs, and whose brother had forgotten the second verse of the song. She let their chatter lift her like a warm tide, yet somewhere below it a quieter current tugged—tender, ridiculous, persistent.

Do not be foolish, she told her heart. *Some joys are meant for others.*

Across the clearing, Noah set his palm upon a fence post to feel its strength and found his thoughts returning, uninvited, to the curve of Naamah's smile when she teased the stars. He shook his head at himself, content and unsettled at once.

Not yet meant, he thought, surprising himself with the shape of the hope, *but perhaps still promised.*

The drum softened to a heartbeat. Under a sky bright with patient stars, the wells kept their vigil, and the wedding feast burned steady as a lamp against a world of growing darkness.

CHAPTER FIFTEEN

THE SIGN AND THE SILENCE

I t began before sunrise, when the air was still and the stars were fading one by one.

Noah had risen early, as was his habit, to fetch water before the camp stirred. The wells glowed faintly in the half-light, the ropes damp with dew. He knelt to pray—simple words, the same each morning, thanking the Almighty for safety through the night and asking for wisdom to keep the people in peace.

The earth answered.

It began as a sound rather than a movement—a low hum, deep beneath the soles of his feet. The jar at his knee quivered; the ropes along the well trembled. Then the ground gave a long sigh and shifted, the stones grinding softly together as if the bones of the world were turning in their sleep.

Noah caught the rim of the well and stayed still, breath held, eyes lifted toward the paling stars. The sound rose, deepened, and passed. The earth did not crack, no tent fell—but every living thing in the camp felt it. Dogs whined, goats bleated, children cried out.

And then—the stillness.

It was the same kind that had come before the Watcher months ago, only this time it felt different—cleaner, almost reverent.

When Noah stood, the dawn was breaking. A line of gold touched the ridge, and from the far hills a flock of birds burst upward all at once, wings flashing like sparks.

Methuselah was already walking toward him, staff steady, eyes bright. The old man's robe brushing the dust.

"You felt it," he said.

Noah nodded. "It was as if the earth wanted to get the attention of man and beast."

"It remembers obedience," Methuselah said quietly. "Long ago, it yielded only to the hand of the Maker. Now it yields to greed and violence, and it groans beneath them." He placed a hand on Noah's shoulder. "Do not fear this trembling. It is a mercy when the ground warns before it breaks."

Others gathered, frightened faces half-dressed in sleep. Lamech called for calm; the women soothed crying children. Tirzah clutched Naamah's hand.

"It was a warning" some whispered.

Methuselah lifted his staff. His voice carried over the murmuring crowd, deep and steady.

"It was a sign," he said. "Not the trembling of earth alone, but a warning to all flesh. The patience of the Almighty is not endless. His heart grieves for the violence and corruption that stain the ground He made, and the day will come when His silence ends."

He turned slowly, his gaze sweeping across the gathered faces—men, women, children clutching at their mothers' robes.

"Let every household remember its Creator," he said. "Let every man weigh his ways. For when the Holy One withdraws His hand, the earth itself will bear witness against those who forget Him."

A hush settled over the camp. Even the animals seemed to listen.

Noah bowed his head, thoughtful, but spoke no word.

Methuselah lowered his staff and added more gently, "Fear not, my children. The Almighty does not warn without purpose. His mercy still stands for those who honor Him."

That night, while the camp settled, Noah sat near the wells alone. The tremor had left the stones with faint new cracks—small, like lines on an aging face. He touched them gently.

"Do You still speak through such things?" he whispered into the quiet. "And if You do... what are You asking of us?"

No voice answered, but a breeze passed through the willows, stirring the branches into a soft rhythm that sounded almost like breath.

From her tent, Naamah watched him—his figure still against the glowing embers, his head bowed, hands resting on his knees. He looked less like a man at rest and more like one being shaped by unseen hands.

Tirzah stirred beside her. "You're watching him again," she murmured, half-asleep.

Naamah flushed. "He's praying."

"Then pray with him," her mother said. "The Almighty hears from both sides of the fire."

Naamah smiled in the dark and whispered her own prayer, one she had not dared speak aloud before. "If You have chosen him, teach me how to walk beside him."

Outside, the wind sighed across the wells. The earth, newly woken, listened.

Chapter Sixteen

THE STRANGER AT THE WELL

B y midafternoon the air trembled with heat. The shepherd boys had driven the goats to shade, and the women moved slowly between the fires, skirts dusted white with flour. From the ridge came a shout—short, uncertain.

"Travelers!"

The word rippled through the camp. Few came that way anymore. Methuselah's people had long been left alone, too poor to plunder and too steadfast to join in the trades of the plains. Yet now, two figures staggered toward them through the shimmer, bent under the weight of thirst.

Noah and several men went to meet them. The strangers were gaunt, their skin cracked from sun and hunger. Dust filmed their eyes. One leaned on the other, whispering words that sounded more like apology than greeting.

Water was brought, and bread. They ate little at first, as starving men do. When they had rested, Methuselah came forward with Lamech and Noah at his side.

"Peace to you," Methuselah said. "You have found shelter. Tell us what brings you to our wells."

The older of the two travelers bowed his head. "Peace, elder. We come from the lowlands near Nod. There is no shelter there now—no peace." His voice was rough, hollowed by travel. "The rivers are poisoned with silt, the fields burned by hands that no longer sow. Men worship the bright ones and offer their sons to them for favor. Those who will not bow are driven out."

Murmurs spread through the listeners. Methuselah's face was grave but calm.

"And your food?" he asked quietly.

"Gone," said the younger man. "We lived on wild roots and berries from the northern cliffs. Red ones—sweet at first, then bitter. They are all that grow there now."

At the mention of berries, Tirzah—who stood behind Naamah—lifted her head slightly, as though she had caught a memory of home.

The elder traveler went on. "We came this way hoping to find honest men still left upon the earth. If there are any, they dwell here."

"You found them," Methuselah said simply. "Eat, rest, and fear no harm."

He turned to the people gathered. "Let us thank the Almighty who still allows strangers to find mercy among us."

That evening, when the heat had softened, Methuselah spoke again to the camp.

"You have heard their words," he said, his staff planted firm in the dust. "The earth beyond these ridges rots in its own pride. Violence fills the hands of men; they forget who gave them breath. We will not answer evil with fear. We will answer it with remembrance."

He looked to Noah. "Gather stones. Tonight we will build an altar to honor the Holy One who still guards His remnant."

By dusk the work began. The men lifted heavy slabs from the dry wash; women fetched water to cool the workers' throats. Naamah carried smaller stones, her palms reddened but her spirit alight. Tirzah worked beside her, humming softly, arranging the rounded stones with a practiced eye.

"It has been long since we built an altar," Naamah said, wiping her brow.

Her mother smiled. "Too long. The world forgets faster than it forgives."

Nearby, Noah directed the men, his calm voice threading through the clatter of stone. Methuselah watched him with quiet satisfaction. "The old ways live again," he murmured.

When the altar stood—a low mound of stone lined with smooth clay—Noah brought the offering: the first grain of the new harvest, mixed with oil. Methuselah lifted his hands over it.

"O Maker of heaven and soil, remember Your servants," he prayed. "Spare the humble, turn the proud to dust. Let this smoke rise as a plea for the world You formed."

He lit the fire. The smoke curled upward, straight and true into the deepening sky. A murmur ran through the people—relief, awe. Naamah felt it too, a hush that reached the marrow. The Almighty was listening still.

After the prayers, the camp settled to eat. The travelers sat close to the fire, their eyes softening with gratitude. They spoke of the roads they had taken—empty markets, idols of stone and gold standing where trees once grew.

Tirzah listened, kneeling by the fire to mend a torn cloth. When they mentioned again the red berries from the northern cliffs, her hands stilled. "How far are these cliffs?" she asked gently.

"Half a day's walk north," said the younger traveler. "The vines cling thick along the streambeds. The fruit lasts even in heat."

Tirzah smiled faintly. "It has been long since we tasted berries here."

Naamah laughed softly. "Perhaps they will grow again when the earth is healed."

"Perhaps sooner," her mother said, eyes distant, thoughtful. "It would please the elder to taste such sweetness."

Naamah didn't notice the quiet note in her voice. She only laughed and handed her a loaf. "You would spoil him like a child."

"Perhaps that is what keeps him young," Tirzah said, but her gaze drifted toward the dark ridge that hemmed the valley.

Later, after the fires died low and the camp lay sleeping, Tirzah lingered outside their tent, the faint scent of smoke clinging to her hair. She looked toward the north where the hills lay faint and blue under the rising moon.

"I'll need a basket," she whispered to herself, the thought blooming like a small, secret joy.

The next morning, she would rise before dawn to fetch what she believed would be a gift of sweetness. The world beyond the ridges had other plans.

CHAPTER SEVENTEEN

THE GIFT OF BERRIES

B efore the first hint of light, Tirzah was already awake.

She moved quietly, careful not to wake Naamah, whose soft breathing filled the small tent. Outside, the camp still slept; even the goats had not begun to stir. The stars lingered, pale and patient, as she filled a small woven basket and covered it with cloth.

Her hands were steady, her heart light. The travelers' words from the night before played in her mind: *"Sweet red berries by the northern cliffs."* She had not seen such fruit in years—not since her daughters were small. The thought of Methuselah's delight made her smile. Perhaps she could make a pie for him, something simple and sweet to mark the mercy they'd been shown.

Just a short walk, she told herself. *I'll be back before the sun crests the ridge.*

She found Sela near the embers of the dying fire, the young woman keeping watch over the last pot of coals. "Tirzah? You're up early."

Tirzah smiled conspiratorially. "I thought to fetch something pleasant for the elder. Do you remember the travelers' tale of berries near the northern stream?"

Sela frowned. "Beyond the markers?"

"Only a little beyond," Tirzah said gently. "You know I'm not one for foolish risks. It will be fine." She touched Sela's arm. "Keep my secret. I want it to be a surprise."

Sela hesitated, caught between respect and worry. "At least take one of the men—"

Tirzah shook her head. "No need. The way is easy, and I'll be back before you've finished tending the fire." She smiled again, motherly and kind. "Don't tell Naamah. She worries more than I."

And with that, she slipped into the dawn.

The valley lay quiet under the waking sky. Dew glittered on the trees; birds began to call in low, sleepy notes. Tirzah walked swiftly, her basket swinging lightly from her hand. The air smelled clean and sharp.

At the ridge, she paused, glancing once behind her. The camp was already hidden by distance. For a heartbeat,

she thought she heard the faint sound of someone calling—but it was only the wind moving through the rocks.

"Just a few handfuls of berries," she murmured. "Then
home again."

She crossed the ridge.

When Naamah woke, the light was full, and her mother's place beside her was empty. She assumed Tirzah had
gone early to the fires, but the morning stretched on and
she did not appear. By midday, unease took root.

"Sela," Naamah called as she passed the cooking fires.
"Have you seen my mother?"

Sela's eyes darted away. "No... not since early."

Something in her tone made Naamah still. "What is it?"

Sela swallowed hard. "She said she was going to gather
berries. For the elder."

"Berries?" Naamah repeated, her voice tightening. "Beyond the ridge?"

"I told her not to go," Sela whispered. "She said she'd
return before the sun rose."

Naamah felt her knees weaken. "That was hours ago."

Without waiting for permission, she turned toward the
northern pass. Sela caught her sleeve. "You can't go alone!"

Noah's voice came from behind them. "She won't." He
had overheard and was already gathering a small group of
men. "We'll bring her home."

Naamah's eyes met his—pleading, fearful. He nodded once, steady and sure. "Stay here. You'll hear my call before you see us."

She wanted to argue but couldn't find her voice.

They found the first sign near the stream: a trail of broken reeds, a piece of woven basket half-buried in mud, and the scattered flash of red berries crushed into the soil.

No one spoke. The forest was wrong—too quiet, too still. Noah crouched, fingers brushing a footprint twice the size of his own. His stomach turned cold.

"Nephilim," he whispered.

Lamech's jaw tightened. "We go slow. Eyes sharp."

They followed the disturbed path for a hundred paces until the smell of trampled greenery gave way to a flash of color that didn't belong. A shawl lay draped over a stone, its edge torn. Noah recognized it instantly—the one Tirzah had worn the day before.

He closed his eyes briefly, offering a silent prayer. "Merciful One, let her be beyond pain."

The others stepped back as he moved forward. It did not take long to find her. She lay half-hidden in the reeds, her face turned toward the sky, peaceful as if asleep. Whatever had struck her had done so swiftly, leaving no cruelty, only stillness.

Noah knelt, trembling, and covered her with his cloak. He bowed his head. "She went out with love," he said softly, "and love will remember her."

The men carried her back before the sun touched the hills.

The camp met them with silence then wails. Naamah's cry broke like something sacred tearing. Methuselah came to meet them, leaning on his staff, eyes dim with sorrow.

"She went to bless another," he said, voice roughened by grief, "and the curse of the world found her instead."

They laid her body not far from the altar built only the night before—the altar where, during its dedication, Noah had placed grain, oil, and a small lamb as offering to the Almighty. Methuselah raised his hands once more and prayed.

"Receive her, O Maker," he prayed. "The earth is no longer gentle, but she was. Let her rest where no violence can reach."

Naamah fell by the altar, her tears falling on the stones, darkening the clay. Noah stood near, his hands trembling, wanting to speak but knowing no words were large enough.

When the prayer ended, Methuselah placed his hand upon Noah's shoulder. "Evil now walks closer than we wished to believe," he said quietly. "But do not let fear be your teacher. Let righteousness be."

Naamah's sobs quieted into shivers. Noah turned to her then, his voice low. "She will not be forgotten."

Naamah looked up at him, eyes rimmed with red, and for the first time did not hide the depth of her grief—or the strength within it. "Then help me remember her well," she whispered.

"I will," he said. And in that promise, something began that neither of them yet understood.

That night no one sang. Even the children were silent, clutching their mothers. The red berries Tirzah had gathered lay untouched beside the fire, their color too bright for mourning.

Above them, the stars blinked coldly, watching a world sliding toward its reckoning. The women prepared the body for burial and the men held vigil overnight.

CHAPTER EIGHTEEN

THE MOURNING AND THE PROMISE

T he morning after Tirzah's death dawned gray and breathless. Even the birds kept to the tamarisks, their songs caught somewhere behind the clouds.

Naamah sat near the entrance of her tent, her mother's shawl gathered in her lap. The fire before her had burned to ash hours ago, but she hadn't moved to rebuild it. Her eyes were hollow from weeping, her face drawn and pale.

The camp was silent except for the dull thud of stones being placed for the grave. No laughter, no children's games—just the slow, reverent labor of love and loss.

Noah worked among the men, setting each stone with care, his hands raw. Every sound of falling earth struck through Naamah's chest like a heartbeat that no longer belonged to her.

When Methuselah came, she did not look up. The old man knelt stiffly beside her, laying a hand upon her head as a father might.

"Child," he said, his voice low, "the Almighty weeps with those who mourn the righteous."

Naamah's lips trembled. "She was all I had."

"You have more than you know," Methuselah said. "She has not vanished—only gone where violence cannot touch her. You will see her again when the world is made new."

Naamah turned the shawl in her hands. "Then I wish the world were new today."

Methuselah's eyes softened. "So do I," he whispered.

By midmorning the grave was ready. Tirzah's body was laid gently in the earth. Naamah knelt beside her one last time, pressing a strand of woven grass across her chest.

"Sleep well, my mother," she whispered. "You've earned your rest."

Methuselah spoke over them, his voice clear and trembling.

"From dust we came, and to dust we return. But the breath given by the Creator is not lost—it only travels home. Let this earth be light upon her, for she was light to all who knew her."

Noah helped Naamah to her feet when the last stone was set. She swayed, exhausted, and he steadied her, not speaking.

When the people drifted away, she remained near the altar, staring at the curling wisp of smoke that still rose from the embers.

"She would have wanted to feed everyone," Naamah said softly. "Even those who took from her."

Noah nodded. "That was her strength. The world will be judged for such things."

She looked up at him then—truly looked. "Why does the Almighty let the wicked live while the gentle are taken?"

Noah hesitated. "Maybe because the gentle have already learned what He meant us to learn. The rest of us still have to be taught."

Her eyes filled again, but her voice steadied. "Then I hope He teaches quickly."

Noah smiled faintly. "He will. In His time."

He started to step away, but she caught his sleeve. "Thank you," she whispered.

"For what?"

"For bringing her home."

Noah looked at her hand resting against his arm, small and trembling, and placed his other hand over it. "It was the least I could do for her," he said. "And for you."

Their eyes held, grief and something tender mingling in the still air between them.

That night, the camp gathered again for prayer. Methuselah spoke little—only that righteousness must not retreat in the face of sorrow. "The earth has grown dangerous," he said, "but holiness must not hide. We will remember Tirzah with obedience, not fear."

When the gathering ended, Noah lingered by the altar. The stars were sharp above him, the air thin and cool. Naamah approached quietly, her steps soft in the dust.

"I brought her shawl, I thought you might keep it until I can bear to."

Noah took it carefully, folding the worn fabric. "It smells of smoke and thyme," he said.

"She used it every day," Naamah murmured. "She said it kept away sadness."

He smiled faintly. "Then perhaps we should share it."

For the first time in days, she smiled too—small, fragile, but real.

Later, when she lay down to sleep, Naamah dreamed of her mother standing on a green hillside, smiling, her arms full of the red berries she had gone to gather. The sky above her was whole and new, and in the dream, there was no fear.

She woke with tears on her cheeks, but the weight on her chest had lessened. The grief was still there, but beneath it something else had begun to grow—a quiet certainty that her mother's love had not ended; it had simply changed its shape.

CHAPTER NINETEEN

THE UNION OF TWO FAITHFUL HEARTS

The weeks after Tirzah's burial drifted by like soft breath over stone. Each dawn came a little brighter, each night a little less heavy. The ache in Naamah's chest remained, but grief had begun to take on a gentler shape—no longer a storm, but a tide that came and went with the wind.

She wore her mother's shawl every day. The threads smelled faintly of thyme and smoke, and sometimes she caught herself pressing the fabric to her face when she thought no one was watching.

Noah often saw her then. He never spoke of it, never interrupted her solitude, but something in him softened each time—the way her eyes lifted toward the sunrise, the way she smiled at the smallest kindnesses, as though relearning joy.

The Season of Healing

One morning she was at the well, filling jars for the cooking fires, when the rope slipped and splashed water up her sleeve. She laughed—an easy, unguarded sound that startled even her. Noah looked up from where he was mending a fence post nearby and caught that laugh. It settled into him like sunlight after weeks of gray.

Later that day, he passed her near the tamarisk trees. She carried a basket of grain; he took it from her hands without asking. "You'll spill half of it trying to carry it that way," he said.

"I was doing fine," she protested, smiling despite herself.

"You were doing bravely," he corrected, and she laughed again, low and warm.

It became like that between them—small things shared without intent, words that lingered longer than they should have. The camp noticed first.

"Naamah," Sela teased one evening as they kneaded dough, "you smile differently when he's near."

Naamah blushed. "I smile the same."

"Not in your eyes," Sela said, and Naamah swatted her with a rag, but her heart fluttered all the same.

The Flowering of Affection

The days grew warmer. Noah spent his afternoons repairing the outer pens with the young men. Naamah often brought water to them, pretending it was duty. From a distance she watched the strength in his shoulders, the quiet patience in his voice.

He was not like the other men—never boastful, never sharp-tongued. He carried authority without effort, as if the ground itself respected him.

One afternoon he looked up and found her watching. Their eyes met, and for a heartbeat, neither moved. Then she turned quickly away, the heat rising in her cheeks.

That night, she lay awake, her heart racing for reasons she couldn't name. She thought of his voice, steady and deep; the way his smile appeared slowly, as though it had to earn its way through his thoughts. The thought frightened her and thrilled her at once.

Mother, what would you say to me now? she whispered into the dark. *Would you tell me to guard my heart—or to listen to it?*

The Confession by the Fire

A few nights later, unable to sleep, Naamah stepped out beneath the stars. The campfires were nearly out; only one still glowed near the altar. Noah sat there, head bowed, his hands resting on his knees.

She hesitated, then went to him.

"I didn't mean to disturb you," she said softly.

"You didn't." He looked up. The light caught in his eyes, deep as river water. "I come here when the world feels too heavy."

"So do I," she said, sitting beside him. The air smelled faintly of cedar and ash. For a moment they said nothing. The night hummed around them, alive with unseen wings.

"I keep thinking of my mother," she whispered. "I thought when she died, my heart had died with her. But lately—" She stopped, afraid of sounding foolish.

Noah turned to her, waiting.

"Lately," she continued, voice trembling, "sometimes it stirs again. When I hear you speak, or when I see you smile at the children... it's as if my heart remembers something it's not supposed to."

Noah's breath caught. "Naamah..."

"I know it's too soon," she said quickly. "I don't mean to shame myself. I only—"

He reached out, covering her hand with his. "Don't be ashamed. The Almighty made our hearts to live, not to wither."

She looked down at their joined hands. "Then perhaps... this is not wrong?"

He shook his head slowly. "Perhaps this is her last gift to us both—that your heart can still feel, and mine can still be moved."

Their eyes met. No words followed, but the silence was full—holy, tender, and alive with a promise neither dared speak aloud.

The Blessing

At dawn, Methuselah stood watching from his tent as Naamah left the altar, her shawl fluttering in the breeze. Noah walked beside her, not touching, yet something between them had changed—the air itself seemed aware.

Lamech joined him quietly. "You see it too?"

Methuselah nodded. "Yes. The Almighty joins light to light, even in a darkening world."

Later that day, he called them both before the camp. The people gathered, smiling, hopeful—everyone had seen this love take root.

"My children," Methuselah said, raising his staff, "you have both known loss and found mercy. You have both chosen faith over fear. The Almighty blesses such a union, for it strengthens what remains of goodness upon the earth. Be joined before Him, and let your lives be a shelter in the storm to come."

Naamah's heart swelled as Noah took her hands. His palms were rough, warm, sure. The world seemed to hush around them.

"I have nothing to offer you but my strength," he said quietly, "and my vow to follow the Almighty all my days."

"And I have nothing to bring but my heart," she whispered, "and the hope that it may always find its home with yours."

Methuselah smiled, tears shining in his ancient eyes. "Then before heaven and these witnesses, you are bound in covenant. What the Holy One joins, let no darkness divide."

The people cheered softly. Sela wept openly. And Noah bent his head, pressing his forehead gently to Naamah's, a gesture both humble and full of promise.

When Methuselah's words fell quiet, the people broke into soft cheers—relieved laughter mingling with tears. E ven in a world grown cruel, there was still cause for song.

Sela clapped her hands. "We'll not end this day with silence!" she cried. "There will be bread and honey, and music if I must beat the pots myself!"

Methuselah chuckled, his old eyes glinting. "Let it be so. If joy is rare upon the earth, then let it sound loudly here."

Within the hour, the camp had come alive. Fires were stoked high, and garlands of woven reeds and wildflowers were hung from tent to tent. Children ran laughing between the stones. The shepherd boys brought out flutes, and someone found a drum that had not been played since the last wedding feast long ago.

The Celebration

Naamah wore her mother's shawl over a simple linen gown. Sela and the other women had adorned her hair with blossoms of the pale desert lily—rare, fragrant, pure white.When she stepped into the circle of firelight, a hush fell over the camp.

"She looks like dawn itself," one of the men whispered.

Noah waited at the center, freshly bathed, his hair tied back, the lines of work and weather softened by the flicker of flame. When he saw her, he could not move for a heartbeat. *This is what peace looks like*, he thought.

They shared a shy smile—gentle, reverent, full of unspoken wonder.

The feast began with laughter and story. Methuselah insisted on sitting among the children so that he might "hear joy up close."The travelers who had once brought tidings of famine now lifted their cups in gratitude that they had lived to see a wedding born of faith.

Bowls of roasted grain, honey cakes, and bread perfumed with oil were passed around. A jar of date wine was opened in Methuselah's honor, and he blessed it with trembling hands.

"For sweetness that endures," he said, "and love that does not forget."

Then came the dancing.

The flutes rose, the drumbeat quickened, and pairs of men and women joined hands around the fire. Naamah hesitated at first—then Noah reached for her hand.

"Will you dance with me?"

She laughed softly. "I thought you did not dance."

"I've had no reason to—until now."

The camp cheered as he drew her into the circle. Their movements were modest, graceful, but the joy between them was unmistakable. The firelight shimmered across their faces, and Naamah's eyes shone brighter than any flame.

When the music slowed, Noah turned her gently toward him, his hands still clasping hers. "I could dance to this heartbeat forever," he whispered.

Naamah's cheeks flushed. "Then you had best keep your strength, husband. The night is long."

He smiled—an expression so rare it stole her breath—and the crowd erupted in laughter and applause.

The Night of Peace

As the stars deepened overhead, the laughter softened to quiet talk and the steady hum of contentment. Methuselah sat watching the newlyweds, his heart full. He leaned toward Lamech. "It does my old eyes good to see love unashamed in this age," he murmured. "It is proof that the Almighty has not yet turned His face away."

Lamech nodded. "They are the beginning of something, Father. I can feel it."

Methuselah smiled faintly. "Then may what begins in joy endure the storm."

When the fires burned low and the music faded, Naamah and Noah slipped away beneath the tamarisk trees, the air cool and fragrant. The moon hung above them like a pale blessing.

"Do you think she saw?" Naamah asked quietly, touching the shawl around her shoulders.

Noah looked upward. "I think she's smiling even now."

Naamah leaned against him, closing her eyes. "Then my joy is full."

He kissed the crown of her head. "And mine," he said simply.

When the laughter faded and the last torch was lowered, Noah took Naamah's hand. The air between them felt new—alive and trembling. She followed him through the curtain of reeds that marked their tent, her heart racing, her breath quick and shallow.

Inside, the firelight flickered over woven mats and a few flowers someone had scattered there. It was quiet except for the soft crackle of the lamp. For a moment they simply looked at one another—husband and wife, still half unbelieving.

Noah reached to brush a strand of hair from her face. "You're trembling," he murmured.

"So are you," she whispered back, smiling through her nerves.

He laughed softly, the sound breaking the stillness. "I've never feared battle or storm as much as I fear the chance of hurting you."

"You won't," she said, taking his hand and pressing it to her cheek. "My heart is already yours."

The world seemed to narrow to the sound of their breathing. He bent his head slowly, giving her every moment to draw back. She didn't. Their first kiss was quiet, unsure at first—then sure, deep with the sweetness of promises kept.

When they drew apart, Naamah's eyes shone. "Is this what it means to belong?"

Noah smiled, his forehead resting against hers. "It means you are no longer alone."

They sat together long after, speaking softly of small things—the scent of the lilies in her hair, the sound of the night outside, the way the stars seemed to burn brighter. When words faded, they rested in each other's arms, hearts steady, peace settling around them like a blessing.

Outside, the camp lay still beneath the moon. Inside, the beginning of their life together took its first quiet breath.

CHAPTER TWENTY

THE DAYS OF EARLY JOY

T he first weeks of their marriage passed in a kind of gentle wonder. The camp had settled back into its rhythm, but for Naamah the days felt newly lit. Every task carried a sweetness: drawing water beside her husband, sharing the bread she baked, hearing his voice call her name in the mornings.

They built their dwelling together near the tamarisks. Noah worked with quiet patience, shaping each beam by hand while Naamah smoothed the clay for the hearth. When evening came, they would sit at the doorway and watch the herds drift home under the pink-gold sky.

Sometimes he told her stories from his boyhood — how Methuselah had taught him to read the stars, how Lamech once sang to call the goats back after a windstorm. She laughed easily, and he would pause just to listen to the sound.

At night they prayed together, simple words of thanks for the day's peace. It amazed Naamah how quickly the sound of Noah's breathing beside her had become the measure of her own rest.

One afternoon, while she pounded grain with the women, Sela teased, "Our Naamah hums now instead of sighing." Naamah smiled, cheeks warm. "I have reason." S ela winked. "And will the Almighty soon give you more?"

Naamah laughed, but her hand drifted to her belly as if her body already held its secret.

As the season turned, small signs of change came to the camp. The herds grew restless, birds flew in strange patterns. Messengers from distant valleys brought news of men building idols to the fallen ones and of violence spreading again through the plains. The peace of Methuselah's people felt like the last still pond before a rising tide.

Noah listened, brow furrowed. "The world is shaking again," he told her one evening. "But I will not let fear take root here."

Naamah took his hand. "We will keep faith, whatever happens beyond the ridges."

He looked at her then with quiet awe. "You have your mother's courage."

"And your patience," she said. "Between us, perhaps we can hold the valley a little longer."

That night the stars burned fiercely above them, bright as promise. Naamah lay awake, one hand resting lightly over her heart, whispering a prayer for the child she hoped would soon come, and for the peace she feared could not last.

CHAPTER TWENTY-ONE

THE BIRTH OF JAPHETH

N aamah's cries broke just before dawn, when the stars were fading and the first pale glow brushed the horizon.By midmorning the camp was alive with movement—Sela rushing for water, Methuselah praying softly at the altar, Noah pacing outside with his hands clenched, helpless and hopeful all at once.

Then the sound came—thin, strong, miraculous. The cry of new life.

When Naamah placed the child in Noah's arms, he thought the air itself changed. The boy's tiny fingers curled around his father's thumb, and Noah felt something pass through him like fire and peace together.

"Methuselah says he will be called Japheth," Naamah whispered, exhausted, glowing. "For he will be enlarged upon the earth."

Noah smiled through tears. "Then let it be so. May he live to see what I cannot imagine."

Methuselah entered the tent, his old eyes full of light. He laid his trembling hands over the child. "Blessed are you, little one. May the breath that fills you be counted among the last of the old world and the first of the new."

The baby stirred, and Methuselah looked at Noah. "The Almighty is not yet finished speaking to our line."

That night, Noah stood outside their dwelling holding Japheth against his shoulder. The stars were bright beyond counting. The child slept, small and warm, his tiny heartbeat steady against his father's chest.

And then the stillness changed. The air thickened, the world hushed. Even the wind seemed to kneel.

A voice—vast and low, neither near nor far—filled the space around him.

"Noah, son of Lamech, hear Me. My Spirit shall not always strive with man, for his thoughts are evil continually. One hundred and twenty years are given for repentance. After that, the floodgates of the deep shall open, and the heavens shall pour forth. Build for yourself an ark of gopher wood. For you have found favor in My sight."

Noah fell to his knees, clutching his child to his chest. The stars blurred above him; tears fell unbidden.

"I am unworthy," he whispered.

But the voice had gone, leaving behind only the sound of the night and the soft breath of the sleeping child.

Naamah came to the tent's entrance, her hair loose, her eyes gentle. "What is it?"

Noah turned toward her, his face pale but resolute. "The Almighty has spoken."

She looked down at the baby, then back at her husband. "And what did He say?"

He gazed at their son. "That he is born into the last days of the world."

Naamah drew near, resting her hand over his. "Then we will live them with faith."

And in the quiet of that night, beneath the unknowing stars, the first steps toward the ark began.

CHAPTER TWENTY-TWO

THE BURDEN
OF THE
CHOSEN

T he morning after the Voice, Noah walked among the tamarisk trees as though the earth beneath his feet had changed. Every stone, every breath of wind felt charged with meaning. He had not slept; the words still rang inside him like thunder held in his chest.

Build for yourself an ark of gopher wood... for you have found favor in My sight.

By mid-day he could keep it no longer. He went to his father's tent.

Lamech sat by the doorway sharpening a small blade, his hands steady despite age. Methuselah was within, praying softly. When Noah entered, both men looked up and saw the weight in his face.

"What has happened, my son?" Lamech asked.

Noah knelt before them. "The Almighty has spoken. He will not strive with man forever. The earth is filled with violence, and He will wash it clean. He has appointed one hundred and twenty years for repentance... and has commanded me to build an ark."

Silence fell—long, heavy, broken only by the hiss of the sharpening stone.

Methuselah rose slowly, leaning on his staff. "Describe what you saw."

"No vision," Noah said. "Only His voice. But the words were sure as breath. The ark is to be of gopher wood, made in rooms, sealed inside and out with pitch. Its length three hundred cubits, its breadth fifty, its height thirty. A window above, and a door in the side. It will carry seed and life when the deep breaks open."

Lamech exhaled, shaking his head. "Three hundred cubits? A vessel greater than any built by men!"

"It must be," Noah said. "For it will hold every creature that breathes, and the remnant of man."

Methuselah studied him for a long moment. "If the Almighty has spoken, then the task is not to question, but to obey. The world mocks what it does not understand, yet obedience is its own proof."

He placed both hands on Noah's head. "You will not be alone. My hands are still strong for counsel, your father's for blessing, and Heaven's for strength."

Drawing the Vision

That evening, Noah knelt in the sand outside the tent. With a long stick he began to draw—lines, curves, measurements whispered under his breath. Naamah came to stand beside him, holding a lamp.

"What are you making?" she asked.

"The pattern of our salvation," he said without looking up.

She lowered the lamp, watching the rough shape take form: the hull rising like a mountain from the sand, the decks marked with careful strokes. Her heart swelled with awe and fear. "So large... and to be built here, in this dry field?"

He looked up at her then, his eyes shining with quiet certainty. "The Almighty has said the waters will come even here."

Naamah's fingers tightened on the lamp handle. "And if none believe you?"

"Then we will still build."

She nodded slowly. "Then I will help."

Gathering the Work

Word spread quickly through the valley—Noah, the righteous man, was building a vessel the size of a city. Some laughed outright; others came out of curiosity. Noah hired all who were willing. Men from the nearby settlements came with carts and axes, eager for coin or meat. He sent them into the high forests for gopher wood, its resin thick and strong, perfect for sealing against water.

Elephants were used to drag the felled trees; oxen pulled the timbers across rolling logs. Noah oversaw every part of the work, measuring, cutting, binding. He devised pulleys of rope and levers of stone, using the slope of the land to lift the heavy beams. At first the men marveled at his skill; later, when the novelty faded, they mocked again.

"What flood, Noah? The sky does not weep!"

He answered only, "The day will come when it will not stop."

Each evening, he mixed pitch over the fires—dark, thick, and fragrant. He brushed it onto the wood until his arms ached, sealing each joint with care. The smell clung to him day and night, a scent Naamah came to love because it meant obedience.

The Preaching

Every Sabbath he left the building to speak in the open fields. Crowds gathered to hear the strange carpenter. His voice was strong but sorrowful.

"Turn back to the Creator who made you! The earth groans beneath your violence. Repent, and live!"

For a time some listened; a few even wept. But the weeks turned to months, the months to years, and the laughter returned. "Preacher of storms!" they called him. "Builder of madness!"

Naamah would watch him from a distance, her heart aching. Each rejection seemed to carve new lines in his face. Yet every morning he rose again, prayed, and returned to the work.

Methuselah often came to stand beside him, staff planted in the earth. "Do not measure success by ears that hear," he said softly. "Measure it by faith that obeys."

The Weight of Time

Years passed. The frame of the ark grew massive, its ribs arching against the sky. From the ridges, travelers could see it gleaming with pitch like a dark mountain on the plain.

Naamah bore two more sons—Shem and Ham—and the camp rejoiced, though the laughter often mingled with unease. The world beyond their valley was changing. Cities rose where men worshiped the fallen ones; cruelty became sport. Those who once worked for Noah drifted away, leaving only a few faithful laborers.

At night, Noah and Naamah would walk together along the hull, their steps echoing on the timbers. "Do you ever doubt?" she asked once.

"I doubt myself," he said. "Never Him."

"And if it truly comes to pass?"

He looked toward the stars. "Then the earth will be washed clean, and perhaps, at last, it will know peace."

Methuselah watched them from his tent, the firelight glinting in his eyes. "So it begins," he whispered. "The last hundred years of the old world."

CHAPTER TWENTY-THREE

THE BUILDING BEGINS

The morning sun struck the valley in sheets of gold, lighting the ribs of the great frame that now sprawled across the plain. From a distance the half-finished hull already looked like a dark hill rising from the dust.

Noah stood atop the scaffolding, a measuring rod in his hand, calling down numbers to the men below. "Thirty cubits to the beam! Mind the line—keep it true!"

The workers moved like ants among the timbers, shouting back to one another over the groan of ropes and the low bellows of oxen. Two elephants strained against a sled laden with gopher logs, their sides gleaming with sweat. Each pull was guided by long calls of song that kept the rhythm steady.

Naamah watched from the ground, her shawl drawn close against the pitch-heavy air. She had begun keeping records—how many cubits finished each month, how much resin stored, how many jars of oil and grain set aside. The work had grown too vast for memory alone. She wrote on clay tablets with a stylus of reed, marking every measure with patience that matched her husband's.

The Labor of Obedience

When the sun climbed high, Noah climbed down to mix more pitch. The tar bubbled in wide clay vats set over the fire, the smell thick and bitter. He dipped a flat board, spreading the resin along the seams until the wood shone black.

Shem and Ham, small but eager, helped by carrying pebbles to wedge between the planks. "You see," Noah told them, "every joint must be sealed within and without. Water finds the smallest crack if you give it time."

Naamah smiled from where she knelt packing grain into clay jars. "Just like doubt," she said.

He looked up at her and nodded. "Yes. Even one leak, and all is lost."

The Gathering of Beasts

As the years lengthened, more animals were trained to the work. The elephants hauled beams; the oxen turned the great capstan that raised the main posts. Donkeys carried water jars from the wells, and tame deer grazed along the edges, unafraid of the noise.

Travelers who passed through the valley often stopped to watch, shading their eyes. "He truly means to finish it," they would whisper. Some laughed, some spat, and a few stayed to earn bread, though none lasted long.

One man asked Noah, "If your God is so mighty, why does He need you to build Him a ship?"

Noah answered simply, "He needs only obedience. The ship is for us."

The man laughed and walked away. But Naamah saw the tremor in her husband's hands when he turned back to the work, and that night she rubbed pitch from his palms until they were clean.

The Household of Faith

Seasons turned. The ark rose higher. Methuselah visited often, leaning on his staff, smiling at the boys. "Each beam you lift," he said, "is another year of mercy added to mankind."

Lamech, older now, came less often but always brought words of blessing. "You have built more than a vessel, my son," he told Noah one evening. "You have built patience into wood."

Naamah tended to the camp as it grew—a small village of tents and sheds for tools and food. She dried fruits in the sun, stored figs and lentils, pressed oil, and learned how to keep seed from mold. She taught the women who remained how to weave nets for carrying hay and to twist ropes of flax strong enough to bind the beams.

At night, when the fires burned low, Noah would draw her close and they would listen to the distant night sounds—the lowing of beasts, the creak of wood settling, the murmured prayers of the old men. "Do you ever wish we had been left alone?" she asked once.

"No," he said quietly. "Only that the world had listened sooner."

The Shadow of Mockery

With every new span of timber, the ridicule from beyond the valley grew louder. Bands of young men came to jeer, shouting up at the workers. "How deep is your sea, Noah? How many tears must you shed to float it?"

Sometimes stones were thrown; once, a torch. But the wind died before the flame could catch. Noah said nothing. He only prayed aloud that their hearts might yet soften.

Naamah wept in anger afterward. "Why do you let them shame you?"

He brushed a streak of pitch from her cheek. "Because their scorn cannot sink what God commands to rise."

A Sign of Favor

Years passed, and one evening as the sun bled red behind the ridges, a light misty rain began to fall—soft, brief. The drops hissed against the hot wood, steaming gently. Noah lifted his face to it and smiled. "See," he said, "the heavens give warnings to those who listen."

Naamah joined him, her fingers twined in his. Around them, the smell of that short rain mingled with pitch, sweet and sharp—a scent that would forever mean hope.

High above, the skeleton of the ark loomed, dark and vast against the twilight, its beams gleaming as if the sky itself had anointed them.

Methuselah, watching from his tent, whispered into the damp air, "So it begins—the mercy before the flood."

CHAPTER TWENTY-FOUR

THE PREACHER OF RIGHTEOUSNESS

The valley had known nearly forty years of building when Noah left it to preach again. The ark already towered like a second hill; its shadow stretched over the fields at sunrise. Every morning the workers heard the ring of his hammer, every evening the sound of his prayer. Now the work would rest for a time while he obeyed the other part of the command—the call to warn the world.

Naamah watched him pack dried fruit and a skin of water. "How far will you go?"

"As far as men will listen," he said. "And farther if I must."

She fastened his cloak and touched the line of pitch that never quite left his hands. "Come back to me," she whispered.

He kissed her forehead. "Always."

Among the Cities of Men

Noah's path wound north toward the river settlements where trade still thrived. He spoke in marketplaces and at well gates, his voice clear above the noise.

"Turn from violence. Return to the Creator before the deep breaks open!"

Some turned their faces away. Others mocked. A few lingered, uneasy, as if the words carried a sound they had almost forgotten—the tone of truth.

One evening, as he preached near the old stone altars of a ruined city, the crowd fell suddenly silent. Shadows moved at the edge of the square—tall shapes, broad-shouldered, their eyes pale as smoke.

The Nephilim had come.

They stepped forward slowly, their presence pressing the air flat. Their leader smiled without warmth. "Noah of the valley," he said, his voice deep as thunder. "Still the builder of wooden mountains? Still crying of judgment?"

Noah met his gaze. "Still the servant of the Most High."

The giant's smile faded. "We know the messengers that walk beside you," he said quietly. "They burn too brightly for mortal eyes."

Noah's heart pounded, but he held his ground. "Then you also know their strength."

The Nephilim inclined his head. "We know their protection. It has kept the old man Methuselah beyond our reach for centuries. Now it shields you. But protection is not forever."

Noah answered, "Neither is defiance."

For a long moment the two regarded each other—the corrupted sons of heaven and the faithful son of man. Then the giants turned away, his followers melting back into the dark like mist. The people who had watched fled in terror.

Noah fell to his knees, breathless. In the silence that followed he felt the unseen watchers draw close—beings of light standing guard. One voice whispered within his spirit, *Fear not. You are seen.*

The Keeper of Testaments

When Noah returned months later, the camp rejoiced. Naamah met him at the gate, tears of relief bright in her eyes. "I knew He would keep you," she said.

Methuselah and Lamech called him into the elder's tent. The air inside smelled of cedar and ancient oil. Scrolls of bark and linen lay bound with cord beside small chests of beaten bronze.

"These," Methuselah said, touching them with trembling fingers, "are the writings handed from father to son since Adam walked the garden—the record of creation, the first promise, the laws of offering, and the telling of the fall. Along with them, the covering garments He gave our first parents. These have passed through our line as witness of His mercy with each one adding his wisdom before passing to the next."

He looked at Noah, eyes bright as water in sunlight. "They will be yours when my days are finished. Guard them. In them the new world will remember the old."

Lamech placed his hand over Noah's. "You are the next Patriarch, my son. May you be worthy of the charge."

Noah bowed his head, overcome. "I will guard them as I guard life itself."

A Glimpse into the Unseen

That night Noah walked alone beneath the half-built ark. The moonlight gleamed on the pitch-dark hull. He felt the hush of the spiritual world pressing close. Between the beams, light moved—shapes of fire and wing that no human eye should have seen. The messengers of God stood like sentinels, silent, watching.

He whispered to Heaven, "I will not fail You."

One of the lights flickered, as if in answer, and the wind rose, cool and strong.

Faith in the Darkness

The next morning, Noah climbed back onto the scaffolding, his sons beside him. "We build for what is coming," he said. "And we preach while mercy still stands."

From the ridge Methuselah watched them, the ancient scrolls resting in his tent. The Nephilim would not cross the boundary where the holy messengers waited, but beyond that line the world was already rotting.

He lifted his staff toward the sky. "May the work of the Lord be blessed."

CHAPTER TWENTY-FIVE

THE GATHERING OF YEARS

The years flowed like a long river, each season carrying the sound of hammers and the echo of prayer. The ark now stood complete—sealed within and without with pitch, its sides smooth as stone and black as night. When the sun struck it, it shone like a great shadow made solid.

Noah ran his hand along the hull and whispered, "It is ready."

Behind him came the laughter of young men. His sons had grown tall and sure: Shem, thoughtful and deliberate; Ham, quick and strong; Japheth, broad-shouldered and kind-eyed. They moved together easily, as if the rhythm of the work had shaped their hearts as well as their hands.

Each had taken a wife—women of courage who had chosen faith over comfort. Their tents now ringed the ark like small stars around a moon. Naamah loved them dearly and taught them the tasks of storing grain and fruit, weaving nets, and tending the herds. In the evenings they sang while the men mended tools by the firelight.

The Signs in the Wild

It was in those years that Noah began to notice the change.

At first, it was only that the flocks multiplied without reason. Then deer appeared at the edge of the clearing, unafraid of the campfire. Soon, creatures that had never been seen so near to man began to wander down from the ridges—bears and foxes, cranes and wild goats, even great cats that lay quietly in the grass watching.

Naamah saw them one morning and caught her breath. "They come as if called."

Noah nodded. "Perhaps they are."

By late summer, the air around the valley felt different—alive, expectant. Birds nested in the rafters of the ark. Turtles crawled up from the streams and rested beneath its shadow. The workers whispered that the beasts had lost their fear of Noah's camp.

Methuselah only smiled when he heard. "The Maker is gathering what is His."

The Household of Faith

Life continued with its small joys. Naamah's hands were always busy—kneading bread, filling jars, soothing aches. In the evenings she sat beside Noah while he carved bits of leftover wood into toys: small birds, an ox, a fish. "They will need such things in the new world," he said. "Children should always have wonder to hold." Speaking faith, hope and expectancy that took root into his family.

When the day's heat faded, the whole family gathered for prayer. Methuselah would lift his frail voice and bless them, the light from the fire trembling on his lined face. Sometimes he would read from the old scrolls, his hands shaking as he traced the words first written by their fathers before the flood of corruption covered the earth.

"These are the treasures of our people," he told the sons. "Guard them well, for soon the world will forget its own beginning."

The Death of Lamech

One autumn evening, the call came that Lamech's strength was failing. Noah and Naamah went to his tent. The old man lay wrapped in linen, his breath thin but peaceful. Methuselah sat beside him, holding his hand.

When Noah knelt, Lamech's eyes opened and a faint smile touched his lips. "My son," he whispered, "you have comforted the ground that the Lord cursed. Finish the work. Lead your sons in righteousness."

"I will," Noah said softly.

Lamech's gaze drifted toward Naamah. "You have been his light." Then he closed his eyes, and his spirit slipped away like a sigh.

They buried him on the hill above the valley. For seven days the camp kept silence, and then the work began again, slower, steadier, as if every hammer stroke was a heartbeat of remembrance.

The Approach of the End

Years turned once more. Methuselah grew frail, yet his mind remained bright. He often summoned Noah to his tent to review the writings and the sacred coverings.

"These will go with you," he said. "They must pass into the new world. Promise me they will not be forgotten."

"I promise," Noah said.

Outside, the sounds of the wild filled the air. From the ridge came the trumpeting of elephants, the cry of eagles, the padding of paws. The beasts gathered more each day, moving as if drawn by a song too deep for men to hear.

That evening, as the sun sank and the shadow of the ark reached their tent, Naamah stood beside Noah and watched the animals grazing peacefully together—the lion beside the lamb, the hawk beside the dove.

"Do you see?" she whispered. "Even the wild things are finding peace here."

He put his arm around her shoulders. "Then let us keep it, while we can."

The wind stirred, carrying the scent of rain though the sky was clear. Above them, the first stars appeared, bright and cold, watching as the appointed days drew ever nearer.

CHAPTER TWENTY-SIX

THE LAST OF THE ANCIENT ONES

T he world had grown very quiet.

Once, distant settlements sent traders through Methuselah's valley; now the roads lay empty. The laughter of strangers, the noise of carts and animals—gone. Only the rhythm of hammers against wood, the lowing of the beasts gathering near, and the soft hum of evening prayer remained.

Naamah often said it felt as though the world had shrunk to the size of their camp. Noah agreed. Beyond the ridges, the earth had forgotten its Maker; within them, faith still lived.

And at the center of it all sat Methuselah—the last link to the first dawn.

A Visit to the Tent of Memories

Noah entered his grandfather's tent carrying a bowl of milk and honey. Methuselah was seated upright, thin as a branch but bright-eyed, wrapped in a robe that smelled faintly of cedar. Around him lay the treasures of the patriarchs: scrolls rolled tight in linen, small chests bound with leather, and at their heart, a folded cloth of pale skins that could be seen faintly in the lamplight.

"Well," Methuselah said, smiling, "I see the flood hasn't come yet. Either the Almighty delays His wrath—or you've measured your cubits wrong."

Noah laughed despite himself. "The measurements are true, Grandfather. Only His mercy is long."

"Ah, that's the better answer," Methuselah said. "Sit with me. I would speak while my voice still remembers how."

Naamah entered with fresh bread and the scent of herbs. "And I would listen while my husband remembers his manners," she teased.

Methuselah chuckled. "Ah, the two of you keep the world from falling apart with nothing but kindness and argument. Sit, both of you."

Stories and Laughter

For a time they simply talked—of the early days when the ark was no more than a sketch in the dust, of the first workers who had believed and the many who had not. Methuselah told how, as a boy, he had seen Enoch vanish into light while the other children chased fireflies.

"Your great-grandfather didn't even say goodbye," he said with a grin. "One moment he was walking; the next, he was gone. I've been preparing my farewells ever since."

Naamah smiled through her tears. "Then you'll have plenty of practice now."

Methuselah winked. "Indeed. I shall make it last until the rain begins."

The Charge of the Patriarch

When laughter faded, he grew solemn. He motioned to the scrolls and relics. "Noah, these are yours now. The record of the beginning, the laws of offering, and the promise of the seed. And here—" he touched the folded skins reverently—"the coverings the Almighty gave to Adam and Eve when they left the garden. They have passed from hand to hand for nearly a thousand years. You will guard them in the ark, so that the new world may remember the mercy that clothed the first."

Noah bowed low. "I will guard them as I guard life."

Methuselah nodded. "And you, Naamah—guard his heart. He will carry the weight of creation, and even a righteous man bends beneath such weight."

She reached for his hand. "I will."

He smiled at her with a grandfather's warmth. "You've done it already."

The Family Gathering

That night all the family gathered at his tent: Shem, Ham, Japheth, and their wives. The old man insisted on tasting a little wine.

"To the new world," he said, raising the cup with shaking fingers. "May it be wiser than the old."

They laughed softly. Ham asked, "Grandfather, will you come with us when the flood comes?"

Methuselah smiled, a distant light in his eyes. "No, my boy. The Almighty has granted me enough years to fill the earth twice over. I will rest before the waters rise. But I will be watching—don't doubt that. I may even complain about your steering if the ark drifts too far north."

Even Noah laughed at that, though his eyes were wet. The tent filled with gentle noise—laughter, sniffles, the sound of old stories retold one last time.

The Passing of the Old World

Seven days later, the rain still had not come, but the sky had taken on a strange, expectant glow. Methuselah lay upon his bed of reeds, peaceful, his hands folded over his chest. Noah and Naamah knelt beside him; the sons and their wives stood close.

"My children," he whispered, "when you hear the thunder, do not tremble. It is only the earth remembering its Maker."

Then his breath slowed, and a smile softened his face. "Tell Adam I kept the faith," he murmured, and was gone.

Outside, a sudden breeze swept through the valley, rattling the reeds of the tents. The beasts near the ark lifted their heads and gave a single, mournful cry. Then stillness returned—deep, absolute.

Noah stood long beside the body. "The world feels smaller," he said quietly.

Naamah slipped her hand into his. "Then we will fill it again, together."

He nodded. "Together."

They buried Methuselah beside Lamech on the hill above the valley. When they returned, a fine mist had begun to rise from the ground, a dew heavier than any they had known. It clung to the pitch-dark hull of the ark until it gleamed like glass.

The family gathered beneath it, their arms linked, their hearts bound by love and by the quiet certainty that time had run its course.

CHAPTER TWENTY-SEVEN
THE WEEK OF WAITING

T he ark stood complete, vast and silent, its sides gleaming with the sheen of dried pitch. Around it the valley lay strangely still. The air had changed—heavy, watchful, like the breath before the first note of a song.

On the morning after Methuselah's burial, Noah rose early and walked the perimeter one last time. Every peg was secure, every seam sealed, the ramp oiled so the animals could climb without slipping. From a distance it looked less like a ship than a mountain of dark wood waiting for a sea that did not yet exist.

The Gathering of the Creatures

By midday the first of the pairs began to arrive in earnest. Naamah saw them from the ridge—deer stepping delicately between oxen, cranes gliding overhead, wolves padding beside lambs without malice. She called for Noah, and together they watched, awestruck.

"They come without fear," she whispered.

"They are led," he answered.

All that day and through the next, the procession continued. Birds filled the air like living ribbons. Small beasts scurried through the grass. Even serpents slid peacefully at the edges, tongues flicking in the dust. The sons guided them into their pens while the daughters-in-law scattered grain and filled troughs with water. It was as if the whole earth was moving toward the ark.

From the surrounding hills, people came to stare. Some laughed; others fled, uneasy. "Look," they cried, "even the beasts obey the madman!"

Noah's voice carried over the noise. "The door of mercy is still open! Come while there is time!"

But no one came closer.

Inside the Ark

Within, the ark was unlike anything the world had seen. It was both ship and home, a world in miniature.

Naamah and the women had hung woven fabrics along the inner walls—soft reed mats and dyed linen that turned the lamplight golden. The floors were lined with planks of smooth cedar to muffle the sound of hooves. Cushions stuffed with wool and dried grasses formed places to sit and sleep.

The "kitchen," if it could be called that, was a corner near the great central beam where clay ovens had been fitted with vent shafts through the side walls. Flat stones served as tables; jars of grain, honey, and dried fruits stood stacked in rows, each sealed with pitch and marked in Naamah's careful hand. Hooks of bronze held dried fish and smoked meat high above the reach of smaller creatures. Even bees had made a hive filled with honey.

For waste, Noah had devised channels—simple troughs lined with clay and lime that led downward to collection pits below, to be emptied and sealed when the time came. Buckets of sand and fragrant herbs stood nearby. "Even the ark must remain clean," he had said, smiling at Naamah's raised eyebrow. "Holiness begins with order."

Water jars—hundreds of them—lined the corridors, their mouths sealed with wax. The family had built racks for cuttings of fruit trees and bundles of seeds wrapped in linen: fig, olive, barley, wheat. Every detail was attended to. They did not know how long the voyage would last, only that it must sustain life until the earth was renewed.

At the heart of the lowest deck, the animals rested—lions beside gazelles, bears beside deer, all subdued by a calm that could only be divine. The soft rustle of their breathing became the ark's first music.

The Family's Vigil

On the seventh day, the skies still held their breath. Noah's sons finished securing the last of the stores; the women checked every jar once more. When evening came they gathered in the upper room where their sleeping mats lay. The air smelled of wood and oil and the faint sweetness of stored grain.

Naamah looked around at the faces she loved—her sons, their wives, her husband—and felt both pride and sorrow. "It feels as though the whole world has moved inside," she said.

Noah took her hand. "Perhaps it has—the part worth saving."

They sat together through the night, talking softly, sometimes laughing. Ham told a story about a stubborn ox that refused to climb the ramp until Japheth bribed it with a melon. And Japheth in return told of the young ram that surely left the print of its ribbed horns on Ham's backside as he bent to wind a rope. Even Noah laughed until tears came.

When quiet returned, Naamah whispered, "Do you think anyone will still come?"

Noah's gaze drifted toward the open door below. "I have prayed they will. But if none do, the Almighty will still keep His promise."

Outside, thunder murmured far away, not yet storm, only warning. The beasts stirred restlessly. A dove cooed from the rafters; an elephant sighed like wind in a cave.

The Closing of the Door

At dawn the first drop fell—small, cold, a perfect sphere that struck the threshold and vanished. Then another. Then the sky darkened, and the sound grew like distant drums.

Noah rose. "It is time."

They walked to the door together. Naamah's heart hammered as she looked out into the gray world. Rain streaked the hills, and though they could not see it, the people who had mocked them were scattering toward higher ground.

Then a sound filled the air—not wind, not thunder, but a deep resonant *boom* that seemed to come from the very heart of the ark. The massive door began to move, slowly, steadily, as if pushed by invisible hands. The family stood watching, awed and trembling.

When it closed, sealing them within, the light from outside faded to a thin line—and then was gone.

Inside, the ark settled into silence broken only by the patter of rain on the roof and the slow breathing of countless living things. Naamah turned to Noah and pressed her face against his chest.

"I'm afraid," she whispered.

He wrapped his arms around her. "Then we will keep busy and breath until we are no longer afraid."

Outside, the waters began to rise.

CHAPTER TWENTY-EIGHT
THE WATERS RISE

A t first, they thought the roar was wind.

Then the earth began to shake.

The rain did not fall in drops any longer; it poured in sheets that hissed against the hull like boiling water. The air was thick, metallic, heavy with the smell of storm and pitch. From somewhere deep below came a grinding sound—the ark's keel straining against the sodden ground, timbers moaning like a living thing.

Naamah clung to Noah's arm as the lamps swung wildly. The beasts stamped and bellowed; birds shrieked from the rafters. "Is it lifting?" she cried.

Noah's face was pale. "Not yet," he shouted over the noise. "The deep is breaking open!"

The floor lurched, throwing them against the wall. A roar like thunder and surf together filled the air as water burst upward from the fissures of the earth. For a moment the whole ark tilted, creaked, then shuddered free. They were afloat. The great ship reeling and bobbing.

The Sound of the World Ending

Inside, darkness pressed close. The lamps had gone out. The only light came from flashes through the upper window, where rain hammered against the pitch-sealed pane.

Outside, the world howled—the cries of men, women, beasts; the tearing of trees; the grinding collapse of mountains. Every living thing was crying out to the Creator at once. Even the sea itself seemed to mourn.

No one in the ark could eat. They sat huddled on the upper deck, arms around one another, every pitch and roll a prayer. Naamah held her hands over her ears, but still she heard the voices—shouts, then silence, then the endless beating of the rain.

Ham whispered, "Are they all gone?" Noah's voice was low. "Not yet. But soon."

The ark rose higher, groaning with every wave. Barrels rolled; the elephants trumpeted in fear; the lions pressed their faces to the bars, their eyes wide. The sons ran to steady what they could, tying ropes, righting jars, whispering to the terrified creatures.

For two days the noise never ceased. Thunder merged with the screaming wind until sound itself became pain. No one slept; no one spoke. They clung to one another and prayed.

The Third Morning

On the third morning the thunder lessened. The light through the small window was gray instead of black. The ark still heaved, but more slowly, rocking like a cradle instead of a battlefield.

Noah lit the lamps again. "We live," he said simply.

They ate a little that day—flat bread soaked in honey, a few dried figs. The taste was like memory; none could swallow much. But even that small meal felt like worship.

Below, the animals began to quiet. The elephants rocked in rhythm with the ark; the lions lay down; the birds huddled on their perches. The air was thick with the scent of hay, damp wood, and life.

Naamah descended to the lower deck to help feed them. She moved slowly, touching each creature as she passed—the trembling of a gazelle, the slow breath of an ox, the stillness of a wolf curled beside a lamb. "Peace," she whispered to them all. "Peace. We are still here." Troughs channeled water. The days were spent tending to the needs of the animals.

The New Routine

By the fifth day they began to find order again. Each son took a watch: Shem to the beasts, Ham to the stores, Japheth to the upper decks. The wives carried water and grain, mended ropes, cleaned the channels. Naamah kept the tally of food and reminded everyone to rest when the storm allowed.

They ate together at dusk, sitting on woven mats in the lamp glow. Sometimes they spoke softly of the world that had been—the hills of their childhood, Methuselah's laughter, the scent of cedar smoke from the old camp. Each memory felt like a star fading behind cloud.

At night, when all was still, the sound of rain became almost gentle. Noah would stand beneath the small window, listening, hand on the beam above his head.

Naamah came to him once and said, "You warned them. You did all you could."

He nodded, eyes on the black water beyond. "Yet my heart mourns for every voice I heard out there. Even the cruel ones. The Almighty's grief must be greater still."

She pressed her forehead to his shoulder. "Then let our faith comfort Him, as His mercy comforts us."

The Silence After the Storm

On the seventh day the thunder finally ceased. Only the steady patter of rain remained. The ark drifted, surrounded by an endless gray horizon. The window showed no land, no tree, only water stretching to the edge of sight.

They stood together—eight souls looking out upon the unmade world.

Shem whispered, "It's as if the earth has forgotten it ever lived."

Noah took Naamah's hand. "Then we will teach it to live again."

Behind them the ark creaked softly, breathing with them, carrying the last heartbeat of creation across the face of the deep.

Chapter Twenty-Nine

THE LONG DRIFT

When the thunder finally ceased, the ark drifted upon an endless gray sea. No land, no horizon—only water and the low groan of timbers that had become their heartbeat. Inside, the world had shrunk to eight souls and a multitude of living things.

Yet, within those walls, life found laughter again.

The Rhythm of Survival

Each dawn began the same: Noah lighting the first lamp, the sons unbarring the lower decks, the women moving through the narrow aisles with buckets of water and baskets of grain. The smell of hay and warm breath filled the air. Birds stirred in the rafters, and the elephants gave their low morning sigh, shaking the ark with each shift of weight.

Noah kept a tally scratched into a plank of cedar. "Forty days of rain," he murmured, "and near three months adrift. We may count a year before we see ground."

Naamah smiled. "Then let that year be full, not empty."

Companions of the Voyage

Shem had found a small monkey that shadowed him wherever he went. The little creature rode his head like a crown, chattering softly while Shem worked. When Shem poured feed into the troughs, the monkey would snatch a kernel, chatter triumphantly, and then drape itself around his head and neck again.

"One day," Ham teased, "that beast will learn to build an ark of its own."

Shem laughed. "If it does, I'll let it feed you."

Naamah had her own companion—a bright green bird that perched on the beam near her head as she worked in the upper deck. She spoke to it daily, and soon it began to mimic her words. When she called, "Peace, little one," the bird would echo back in a perfect, piping voice, "Peace, little one," which delighted everyone except Ham, who once spilled a bucket when it startled him from behind.

The laughter that followed echoed through the hull like sunlight.

Japheth's wife, Tirzah, adored the big cats. She carried the lion cubs about as if they were infants, one tucked beneath each arm. The family loved to watch her parade down the passageway, the cubs batting at her braids. Each night Noah would have to remind her gently, "The mothers are calling for their young, daughter."

"But they're so warm," she protested, smiling.

"So are the mothers," Naamah said, laughing.

Even the grim days brightened when the cubs mewed at the sound of her voice, or when the monkey tried to steal Shem's hammer, or when Naamah's bird repeated a line of prayer and everyone fell silent, hearing their own words returned to them like a blessing.

Life Aboard the Ark

Weeks became months. The family learned the rhythm of feeding and cleaning, of soothing restless beasts, of scraping the lime channels and gathering herbs from the soil boxes Shem tended. The air was thick but not unpleasant—wood, oil, grain, and life.

When the day's work ended, they gathered near the vented hearth where a small fire burned blue and steady. Naamah would spread soft reed mats and pour water flavored with honey and mint. They ate simply—flat bread, figs, and the occasional fresh egg from the hens that had taken to laying in unlikely corners.

One evening Ham began to mimic the monkey's chatter so perfectly that even Noah laughed until tears came. The sound filled every deck, rising above the hum of the animals. It felt almost like a festival.

Small Miracles

New life appeared among them—a kid born of the goats, a pair of doves hatching in their nest, seedlings pushing from the soil boxes. Naamah called them *signs of mercy*. "If life can grow here," she said, "then it will surely return to the world outside."

Sometimes she would open the small window to let her bird fly short circles before returning to her shoulder, repeating softly, "Peace, little one. Peace." It became the ark's song.

The Weight of Waiting

After long months adrift, Noah's board of notches stretched beyond counting. They stopped asking *how long* and began asking *how faithfully*. The waiting itself had become their act of worship.

At night, when the lamps burned low, Naamah would rest her head on Noah's shoulder and whisper, "Do you think the earth remembers us?"

He smiled faintly. "Perhaps it dreams of us, as we dream of it."

They would sit in the hush, surrounded by sleeping sons and daughters, by the slow breathing of beasts, by the steady rhythm of wood on water. It was a kind of peace they could never have imagined in the old world.

The Promise of Light

Then one morning, after nearly a year upon the waters, the sky thinned to silver and gold. Noah climbed to the window and drew in a breath of air that smelled faintly of soil. "The wind has changed," he said. "The earth is remembering itself."

Naamah stood beside him, the green bird on her shoulder repeating softly, "Peace, little one. Peace."

He took her hand. "Soon," he said. "Soon the door will open."

And as the ark drifted beneath a widening sky, laughter and hope mingled with the sounds of life—the chatter of the monkey, the purr of the cubs, the whisper of Naamah's bird—as the new world waited just beneath the waves.

CHAPTER THIRTY

THE BIRDS AND THE WAITING

After long months adrift, the sky began to change. The light was softer now, the clouds higher, the air faintly sweet—as if the sea itself had begun to remember the scent of land.

Noah rose before dawn to climb to the small window in the upper deck. When he unlatched it, a rush of clean air filled the ark. For the first time in almost a year, it smelled of earth.

"Come," he called. "See what mercy looks like."

Naamah and the sons gathered near the window. Far to the north, the surface of the water shimmered different-ly—less motion, a hint of shadow just below the waves.

"Could it be mountains?" Japheth whispered.

"Perhaps," Noah said. "But we will wait for proof."

The Raven and the Dove

He brought forth a raven first—black-feathered, restless, strong. It perched on his arm, its head cocked as if already impatient to leave.

"Go," Noah said softly, "and see if the earth has found rest."

The raven burst into the sky, a dark shape against the light. They watched until it vanished into the clouds.

For days afterward, the family waited. The raven did not return to rest in the ark but circled endlessly, feeding upon the waters, a lonely sentinel of the flood's retreat.

Then Noah released a dove. It flew straight and true, small and white, a fragile hope against the vast gray. Naamah whispered a prayer as it vanished into the haze.

When it returned that evening, its feathers were wet, its eyes bright but empty of news. Naamah took it gently in her hands. "Not yet," she said.

They waited seven more days. The ark rocked lazily now, the sea quieter, the beasts calm. The brothers cleaned the pens, scrubbed the troughs, and argued in the way only brothers could.

The Strain of Waiting

"You've taken my shovel again," Ham complained, wiping sweat from his brow.

"It was by the grain bins where you left it," Shem replied evenly.

"I left it *clean*," Ham shot back, "and now it smells like lion."

Japheth laughed. "That may be because you feed the lions."

Ham threw him a glare. "When we reach land, I'm finding my own mountain to live on."

"You'll be lonely in a week," Shem said. "You'll miss having someone to blame."

Even Noah, hearing them from the upper deck, smiled. "If this ark had more space, you'd only argue louder to fill it."

Naamah shook her head. "You'll see," she teased, "when we step on dry ground, each of you will pretend you never liked one another at all."

Ham grinned. "At least the animals don't talk back."

From the beam above them, Naamah's green bird piped, "Peace, little one," and everyone burst out laughing.

The Olive Leaf

Another seven days passed. The ark had settled in a gentle rocking motion, no longer drifting wildly. Noah released the dove again, and they watched it fly into the gold-tinged sky.

The day stretched long. Every creak of the hull sounded like a heartbeat. Naamah found herself pacing; the sons wandered from deck to deck, restless, counting jars, tightening ropes that needed no tightening.

When the evening light dimmed, a fluttering of wings echoed from the window. The dove returned—and in its beak was a fresh, green olive leaf.

Naamah gasped. "Life!"

The others crowded around, silent for a heartbeat, then laughter broke out, unrestrained and joyful. Ham lifted the little bird high. "You see? Even the sky grows trees now!"

Noah took the leaf gently, his eyes bright. "The waters are retreating. The Almighty has not forgotten us."

They placed the olive sprig beside Methuselah's scrolls and bowed their heads in thanks.

The Tension of Hope

The waiting grew harder now, not easier. Hope itself was heavy. Every hour they looked toward the window, longing for land. Even the animals sensed it—restless, pawing the floors, calling out into the still air.

One afternoon, after another small quarrel over water jars, Japheth's wife sighed and said, "When we step on dry ground, I swear I'll walk a mile without hearing any of your voices."

Naamah laughed. "Make it two. I'll walk beside you."

Even Noah smiled. "Just don't wander too far," he said. "We may have to start this whole world over again."

That night they ate together and told old stories. The monkey perched on Shem's shoulder tried to steal Ham's bread. Tirzah's lion cubs purred at her feet, and Naamah's bird chirped softly, "Peace, little one. Peace."

The laughter rose and faded, replaced by quiet wonder. They were still floating between worlds—the old destroyed, the new not yet born.

The Promise of Dry Ground

Seven more days. Noah opened the window once more and released the dove a third time. This time it did not return.

He stood for a long while in silence, Naamah's hand resting on his arm.

"She has found a place to rest," Naamah whispered. "Then so shall we."

The others gathered, hushed, hearts full of awe and impatience.

"Soon," Noah said softly, "the door will open, and the world will begin again."

The ark rocked gently beneath them, like the breath of a sleeping giant, waiting for the word that would wake it.

CHAPTER THIRTY-ONE

THE DOOR OPENS

The ark had come to rest.

No one knew how long it had been drifting when the great groan finally stopped. At first, they thought it another storm, but then the tilting steadied, the waves softened, and the floor lay level beneath their feet.

Days passed. The air through the window grew warmer, touched with the scent of wet stone and leaves. Birds perched on the sill now, bright and curious. The water still stretched far, but in the distance faint shapes had begun to rise—mountains half veiled in mist.

Noah ran his hand along the cedar wall. "She has grounded," he said softly. "The Almighty has set us down."

Naamah stood beside him, eyes shining. "May we praise him upon dry ground soon."

The Command to Go Forth

One morning the light outside changed. Clouds thinned, and a shaft of sunlight fell across the deck, golden and pure. The family gathered instinctively—the sons, their wives, and Naamah with her green bird on her shoulder. Even the animals seemed to sense it; the monkeys chattered, the elephants lifted their trunks toward the light.

Then came the voice—not thunder, not wind, but a deep peace that filled the air.

"Go forth from the ark, you and your wife, your sons and their wives.Bring out every living thing with you, that they may breed abundantly on the earth,and be fruitful, and multiply."

Tears blurred Noah's vision. He turned to Naamah, who nodded. "It is time."

The Opening of the Door

They descended to the lower deck where the great door stood sealed with pitch. Noah placed his hand upon it, closed his eyes, and whispered, "Thank You for the life You have kept."

Then, with a deep breath, he drew back the great bolts. The ramp slowly but loudly creaked downward ending with a solid thud.

Light poured in—white and dazzling after so long in shadow. Warm air rushed through the ark carrying the scent of grass, rain, and growing things. The family shielded their eyes, laughing and crying at once.

The animals stirred first. The doves burst upward through the opening, a sudden cloud of white. Deer followed, bounding down the ramp to the wet ground. Then came the larger beasts—bears, oxen, elephants—moving slowly into the new world. Even the lions hesitated for a moment, blinking at the sun before stepping out into the gleaming green.

From the doorway, Noah watched them go. "See," he whispered, "the earth is alive again."

Joy and Awe

When at last the last creature had gone, they stepped out together—eight souls blinking against the light. The air was cool and sweet, the ground soft beneath their feet. All around, the mountains glistened with streams pouring down their sides, and in the distance the sky arched clear and blue for the first time in their memory.

Ham laughed aloud, stretching his arms. "I had forgotten how wide the world is!"

Shem knelt and scooped up a handful of soil, letting it crumble through his fingers. "It even feels different—clean."

Japheth breathed deeply and said, "If anyone snores tonight, I'll sleep a mile away."

The others laughed, the sound ringing across the silent valley. For the first time in a year, laughter carried without echo.

Naamah bent and pressed her palms to the ground. "Welcome," she whispered to the earth.

The First Altar

Before evening fell, Noah gathered stones from the hillside and built an altar. Naamah brought wood still fragrant with pitch, and together they arranged it carefully. When Noah lit the fire, the smoke rose straight and sure into the quiet sky.

The family stood around it, their faces warm in the glow. The animals grazed in the distance; the sun dipped low. Noah lifted his voice:

"O Lord, You have preserved life through judgment .May this smoke rise as a promise of gratitude.Bless the ground beneath our feet and the children of our children yet to be."

As he finished, a stillness settled over them. Then the sky brightened again—not with storm but with light. Colors shimmered across the clouds—red, gold, violet—spanning the whole horizon like the curve of a hand.

Naamah gasped. "A bow of light and colors!"

Noah smiled through his tears. And the Creator spoke aloud "I have set my rainbow in the clouds and it will be the sign of the covenant between me and you, and every living creature, and the earth, that all flesh will never be destroyed again by flood."

They stood together, awed and silent, as the rainbow burned against the fading sky.

The Night of Peace

That night they camped beside the ark, the smell of grass and clean soil all around them. The stars seemed closer than before, their reflections trembling in the new streams. No one spoke for a long while; words felt too small.

At last Naamah said softly, "It feels strange to breathe open air again."

Noah took her hand. "It feels like the first breath of the world."

She smiled. "Then tomorrow we begin again."

He nodded, looking toward the distant horizon. "To-morrow."

The rainbow lingered long after the sun had set, its colors faint but steady over the sleeping earth—a silent promise that mercy endures beyond judgment.

CHAPTER THIRTY-TWO

THE FIRST MORNING

T he first dawn of the new world broke with a hush.

Mist rose from the valleys, and sunlight spilled like molten gold over the mountain ridges. The air was clean, tasting of water and stone and growing things. The ark lay behind them, settled on the slope, its black hull gleaming in the light like a monument to mercy.

Noah and Naamah stood hand in hand, watching as the day unfolded.Around them, their sons and daughters-in-law moved quietly—checking the grazing animals, gathering fruit from the tender shoots that had sprung overnight. Everywhere there was life.

"It's hard to believe," Naamah whispered, "that the earth can be this beautiful again."

Noah smiled. "Judgment was fierce, but mercy is fiercer still."

She leaned her head against his shoulder. "We have lost much."

He turned to her. "And yet, what remains is everything that matters."

A Family Rekindled

As the sun climbed higher, laughter echoed through the clearing. Ham had found a cluster of figs and was boasting of his discovery until Shem and Japheth tackled him to the ground, scattering fruit and pride alike. Their wives joined in, clapping and cheering, and even Naamah laughed until tears sparkled in her eyes.

"Do you hear them?" she said. "Laughter and joy has returned and the world is young again."

"It is," Noah replied.

The sons worked side by side, gathering stones to build their dwellings. The women spread woven mats and unpacked what they had saved: jars of grain, seeds wrapped in linen, small tools and pottery. It was humble, but it was a beginning.

Naamah knelt in the fresh soil, pressing her palms against it. "It feels alive," she murmured. "Ready."

"Then plant," Noah said gently. "For all that we lost, life begins again with your hands."

She smiled and began to work, her bird perched nearby, repeating softly, *"Peace, little one. Peace."*

The Overflow of Love

That evening, when the sky burned orange and violet, the family gathered by the stream. The animals drank nearby; the air hummed with the sound of creation breathing again. Noah built a small fire, and they ate together—fruit, grain, and honey from the stores they had carried through the flood.

When the meal was finished, Naamah rose. The firelight caught her hair, turning it to bronze. She looked at her sons and their wives, her voice soft but sure.

"You have seen destruction," she said, "and you have seen mercy. Hold to mercy. Love one another fiercely, for it is love that has carried us through the waters."

Shem nodded, his eyes glistening. Ham reached for his wife's hand, and Japheth smiled, quiet and thoughtful.

Then Naamah turned to Noah. "There is one more gift from the Almighty," she said, eyes shining. "One I did not tell you of before."

Noah studied her face, confusion giving way to dawning joy. "Naamah—"

She took his hand and placed it over her heart. "Life has begun again within me."

For a moment he could not speak. Then he laughed—a sound of pure wonder that filled the valley. He drew her into his arms, holding her as though she were the promise itself.

"A child," he whispered. "Born into the new earth."

She nodded, smiling through tears. "The Almighty has remembered us."

The others rose and gathered close, their joy spilling over in laughter and praise. Even the animals seemed to sense it; the dove that had returned with the olive leaf circled once above them and vanished into the glowing sky.

The Covenant Remembered

As night fell, they sat beneath the fading colors of the rainbow that still lingered faintly across the horizon. The air was cool, and the stars glittered like diamonds scattered upon black silk. Noah's hand remained entwined with Naamah's.

"We will teach our children what the old world forgot," he said quietly. "That love is stronger than fear, and obedience sweeter than pride."

Naamah rested her head against his shoulder. "And that even after the storm, joy can be born again."

They watched the heavens in silence, the rainbow fading into starlight, the fire crackling low. The world was new, and hope had taken root again—in soil, in heart, in the tiny life stirring within Naamah.

"While the earth remains, seedtime and harvest, cold and heat, summer and winter, day and night shall not cease."— *Genesis 8:22*

EPILOGUE — THE SONS OF NOAH

I n the years that followed, the valleys grew green ag ain. The rivers cut new paths through soft soil, trees spread their branches, and the earth once more rang with the sound of children's laughter.

Noah and Naamah lived to see the promise fulfilled—sons and daughters, grandchildren, and nations yet unborn. The rainbow often stretched above their dwelling, a reminder that mercy still watched over the world.

Shem, the firstborn, built his tents in the east, where the rivers met the rising sun. His children became the peoples of faith and learning—the Hebrews, the Persians, and those who would one day carry the promise of Abraham. From his line came prophets and kings, and ultimately, the One through whom the covenant would be completed.

Ham journeyed south to the warm lands where palms and rivers thrived. His descendants spread across Africa and parts of Arabia, skilled in building and rich in song and story. Through his line rose mighty nations along the Nile and the coasts of Canaan.

Japheth, the youngest, traveled north and west, following the mountain winds to broad plains and distant seas. His children became the seafaring and the wanderers—Greeks, Medes, and peoples of the far isles. They carried with them the memory of the flood and the dream of freedom beneath open skies.

Thus the sons of Noah were fruitful and multiplied, and from their families came all the nations of the earth.

AUTHOR'S NOTE

This story is a work of fiction wrapped around truth. Written with deep reverence for the Holy Scriptures. While the dialogue, settings, and daily details are imagined, to bring the ancient world to life, the heart of the tale remains true to the Word of God: that faith, obedience, and love can preserve life even through the greatest storm.

May this retelling inspire readers to look upon the story of Noah not only as a record of judgment, but as a testament of grace—a reminder that even when the earth trembles and waters rise, God's promises stand firm, and love endures beyond the flood.

"And God remembered Noah..."— Genesis 8:1